Lyric Novella

T0079858

THE
SEAGULL
LIBRARY OF
GERMAN
LITERATURE

ANNEMARIE SCHWARZENBACH

Lyric Novella

TRANSLATED BY LUCY JONES

WITH AN AFTERWORD BY ROGER PERRET

LONDON NEW YORK CALCUTTA

This publication has been supported by a grant from
the Goethe-Institut India

swiss arts council
pr helvetia

The original edition of this publication was supported by a grant
from ProHelvetia, Swiss Arts Council

Seagull Books, 2022

First published in German as *Lyrische Novelle*
by Annemarie Schwarzenbach (Lenos Verlag, Basel, 1933)

First published in English translation by Seagull Books, 2011

English translation © Lucy Jones, 2011

Published as part of the Seagull Library of German Literature, 2022

ISBN 978 1 8030 9 037 5

British Library Cataloguing-in-Publication Data
A catalogue record for this book is available from the British Library

Typeset by Seagull Books, Calcutta, India
Printed and bound by WordsWorth India, New Delhi, India

CONTENTS

TRANSLATOR'S INTRODUCTION

Pantomime and seedy theatre halls, with their cross-dressing, make-up, false eyelashes and false breasts, have long been an attractive backdrop for writing on the theme of gender ambiguity. Theatre halls have also been places for class distinctions to blur, relax, be played with; for women to steal clandestine glances at men, men at women, women at women and men at men. They are the perfect locations for voyeurism: everyone is meant to gaze at the actors on the lit stage, watch the movements of bodies framed in certain cuts of cloth, smell sweat and face paint.

Two writers, Christopher Isherwood and Annemarie Schwarzenbach, who lived in Berlin in the early 1930s, wrote about their experiences in a more or less fictionalized form in which theatre reflects the tension due to the imminent war as well as the emotional state of the writers. Isherwood's collection of short stories, later published together as *The Berlin Stories*, which provided the inspiration for the Broadway musical (1966) and later film, *Cabaret* (1972), centred on the legendary Kit Kat nightclub. The female lead in the film, Liza Minelli, is not a classic feminine beauty to be looked at but not touched; instead, she plays a racy singer wearing little but a corset and suspenders, topped with a bowler hat. Both sexes come together in her stage outfit, and her stage personality, as she rasps in one of her songs, 'is a tiger, not a lamb, Mein Herr'.

Weimar-era Berlin was a place for writers and artists to experiment and broaden their horizons: Isherwood, stifled by his British upper-middle-class background, was fascinated by Berlin's erotic underworld and the freedom it offered him to live out his homosexuality. There are no traces of guilt in his hedonistic tales: 'I am a camera with its shutter open, quite passive, recording, not thinking' ('A Berlin Diary, Autumn Diary, 1930' from *Berlin Stories*). Schwarzenbach, suffocated by her mother's love and tasting bohemia for the first time in the company of Erika and Klaus Mann, was drawn to Berlin for similar reasons, experiencing there the first opportunity to openly live out her sexual identity. *Lyric Novella* also forages into the underworld of dive bars and illicit relationships. But it is a lot less straightforward than Isherwood's romp through the city of Berlin. For Schwarzenbach, entering the heady world of getting what she wanted after many years of moral guilt and repression meant that she found the transition difficult, if her 1933-published *Lyric Novella* reflects her state of mind during this period. She was often melancholic, confused and plagued with guilt. Roger Perret's Afterword goes into detail about the circumstances surrounding her Berlin period: certainly, Schwarzenbach's mind was befuddled, perhaps by her first experiments with morphine, her wild behaviour causing her to spiral into self-destructive habits while she struggled to fulfil opposing demands: those of her family and her own desires. Her narrator in *Lyric Novella*, a nameless young man, struggles with his love for the aloof *varieté* singer Sibylle. He doesn't find release in desire: it presents a spiritual crisis. The young man receives some advice from Erik, a father figure and former lover of Sibylle:

> He told me that you had to realize some essential things
> in life: this had nothing to do with social prejudices but,

in the first place, with our soul, with our dependence on God. I was prepared to accept this and felt very guilty. But I am only human and it was all very well for him to say. He said the greatest sin was to divert one's energy away from God and to toss it into a void. No act of will or sacrifice was justified if not done for the greater good and towards fulfilment of one's true form.

'How do I know my true form?' I said.

'You have to believe that God loves you,' said Erik. 'Then you won't do anything beneath you.'

After Sibylle fails to reciprocate his feelings, the young man goes into self-imposed exile in the country, comparing himself to Michel in Gide's *The Immoralist*:

I am like him, loaded with a similar guilt, at the mercy of a hostile, imaginary and futile freedom.

The reference to Gide is no coincidence: Michel is torn between social convention and homosexuality. For, as Schwarzenbach revealed after the book's publication:

I should have admitted more plainly [. . .] that the hero was not a hero, not a young man, but a young woman.

So is it the consequence of dallying with lesbianism that this young 'man' is afraid of? The costs, either real or imagined, of loving the wrong person—another woman, or the wrong sort of woman—are made clear: being cut off without a penny and dying an ignominious death.

The sober eye of higher moral authority, Our Father, is paralleled by the authority of the narrator's actual father, who is in far-off Russia, seeing to some 'big oil drillings'. Here, as elsewhere, the father does things that are unambiguously and reassuringly male: shooting practice with his son, buying cars and paying for the son's studies and lifestyle. The mother, interestingly, is never mentioned at all. Instead, the atmosphere in Schwarzenbach's book is constantly foreboding, and the young narrator is running scared from an imagined castigator, or perhaps even himself:

> Forgive me, it's just that I've been expecting some terrible danger to happen for days now.

The book is a portrayal of his unravelling.

Emancipation from his family eludes him, even in the big city; despite the hedonism of the theatre, the long night drives and illicit dives full of criminals, his relationship with the experienced, older Sibylle remains chaste: there is not one kiss, not one erotic scene except for a dream. But all the while, he casts her furtive, sidelong glances. The mere thought of actually succumbing to his desire makes Schwarzenbach's young man break out in a sweat, become chronically ill, fear for his life and hallucinate. The few descriptions of physical contact are therefore electrifying: a touch of Sibylle's hand to his forehead, her cheek against his, her hand on his shoulder. One suspects that there is, in fact, nothing in this young man's trousers, that he must be a child wanting a mother. Or that there is something much more troubling and psychologically terrifying going on here: a void opening up to swallow him, made up of terror of his (or her) own erotic identity. Another woman, Irmgard, appears briefly on the scene, a lady of proper standing who it seems could solve all problems with her 'candid, gently seductive, intense expression' and a less threatening mix of good breeding and adventurousness. But her inauspicious surname, Frau von Niehoff (literally, 'of no hope') proves prophetic: Irmgard ends up taking care of the young man like a little child, tending to him when ill and tucking him up in 'linen . . . [that was] wonderfully cool and lightly scented with toilet water'.

In her review of Alexis Schwarzenbach's *Auf der Schwelle des Fremden*, Franziska Bergmann writes: 'The few or missing gender classifications of Schwarzenbach's figures can be found . . . in other texts by the author.' Bergmann argues that Schwarzenbach is employing a narrative technique that is 'less about the attempt to fit the female narrator into the heterosexual standard in order not to endanger publication' and more to do with 'the questioning of traditional gender boundaries themselves'. Bergmann goes on to say that, in the light of 'gender-critical' contemporary novelists, such as Jeanette Winterson, this writing technique could be regarded as 'highly avant-garde'.[1]

On this level, the ambiguity of the narrator's gender adds another layer to the text: it opens up a parallel world for the reader, doubling rather than reducing the possibilities of interpretation: it is either the story of a young man's autumn love affair with an unsuitable woman—or a lesbian affair. It allows mothers to be swapped for fathers, male lovers to stand in for female ones. One reading does not inhibit the other but adds to the levels of meaning. And it certainly does not signify the writer's fear of speaking out: in real life, Schwarzenbach made no secret of her homosexuality. Nor was she cut off, either emotionally or financially, by her family, although her behaviour led to a great deal of conflict at home. In contrast to her narrator's father obsession, Schwarzenbach's own father barely made an impression, whereas her mother, an overbearing, jealous woman who manipulated her daughter's life, encouraged the young Annemarie to dress up as a boy well into her late teens. The adult Schwarzenbach adopted an androgynous style of dress for the rest of her life.

Schwarzenbach's real-life restlessness and constant travelling was undoubtedly a flight forward from her mother's control. She too, like the young man in *Lyric Novella,* spent her life fleeing and trying to find solace, often in foreign places and nature. Chaste and in solitude, the young man in *Lyric Novella* writes about the story of his failure to dare to love Sibylle openly; however, peace eludes him and he turns to loathing himself 'because I have no obligations'. Removing himself from his obsession does not remove the obsession itself but leads to another kind of self-torment. The paradox of Schwarzenbach's obsessive travelling throughout her life was that it represented the promise of freedom and being in control, by literally putting herself in the driving seat. But, much like the narrator in *Lyric Novella*, she had her emotional turmoil packed in her luggage.

Note

1   Franziska Bergmann, 'Neue Erkenntnisse für die Annemarie-Schwarzenbach-Forschung'. Available at www.zag.-uni-freiburg.de/fff/zeitschrift/band_23/-sport-bewegungen-geschlecht.html (last accessed on 4 January 2011; link no longer valid).

Lyric Novella

One

This town is so small that after one walk, every corner is familiar. I have already discovered an old, very pretty courtyard behind the church, and the best barber here who lives in a cobbled side street. I walked a few paces from his shop and I was suddenly on the edge of town: there were just a few red-brick villas, and a street that was sandy and looked like a cart track. Beyond this began the woods. I turned around, went back past the church and already knew my way around very well. The old courtyard leads you to the main street, and now I am sitting in the cafe Zum rotem Adler to write for a while. In my hotel room, I am always tempted to throw myself down on the bed and spend the brief hours of daylight idle. It requires great effort for me to write as I have a fever and my head is pounding as if from hammer blows.

I think if I knew someone here, I would soon lose my composure; but as it is, I don't speak a word to anyone, and walk around unclear about my emotions.

The cafe seems quite an odd place to me. It appears to be a patisserie, with cakes displayed in vitrines and a shop girl wearing a black woollen dress and a white apron. In the corner, there is a light blue tiled stove, and sofas with upright, cushioned backrests lining the walls. A young puppy runs around yapping loudly, an unkempt, wretched creature. A grey-haired woman tries to stroke him but he runs away from her, his back arched in fear. The old woman follows him, coaxing him with a lump of sugar and speaking loudly to him all the time.

I think she is insane. No one in the cafe seems to take any notice of her.

I have only written two pages so far and the pains are already beginning again, stabbing pains in my right side that cease as soon as I lie down or drink strong liquor. But I don't want to lie down. I could write so well now, and it makes me terribly low to be so idle and all alone.

The insane old woman has left. I'd like to see how she crosses the street and if she talks aloud to herself outside too, like the grey-haired beggar women in Paris.—

I never used to be able to tell the difference between insane people and drunkards; I would watch them in a kind of awestruck horror. But I'm not afraid of drunkards any more. I have often been drunk myself; it is a beautiful, sad state in which we gain clarity on many things we would otherwise never admit to ourselves, emotions that we seek to hide, and that are not the worst in us after all.—

I feel a little better now. I ask the reader to forgive me for what I write today; nevertheless, Sibylle said that even the bitterest experiences and the forlornest hours in my life shouldn't be completely futile. This is why it's so important to me, even in this hopeless state, to give in to

Four

'Mankind is to be pitied,' says Strindberg. Some months ago, I was sitting with a writer in a Berlin coffeehouse. We were talking animatedly, and becoming more and more excited to find we had so much in common. He was a lot older than I was; in fact, I could almost have been his son. He leaned across the small table and held my hands tightly, his elation, his optimism, his rapture almost scorching me like flames. 'You,' he said, 'are youth—and the only youth I don't resent for the future and for triumphing over us—'

His words had a slightly sobering effect on me. He seemed to instantly sense this, let go of my hands, looked at me insistently and said:

'Do you have any idea how charming, and how in danger you are? You are suddenly quite pale. Tell me what I can do to help you.'

I am often being told I'm in danger, perhaps because I am still so young.

But at the time, I laughed about it. 'I adore danger,' I said, feeling pleasure radiating from my eyes.

'Now I must go,' I added. It was midnight and I left him hastily, almost without saying farewell. At the door, it struck me that I'd behaved clumsily, so I rushed back, squeezed his hands and said, 'Forgive me, it's just that I've been expecting something terrible to happen for days now . . .'

'Go on,' he said, smiling, 'face it.'

But I didn't face it.

Five

I was in the woods all afternoon. First, I walked against the headwind across a large field. It was exhausting, I froze, and the edge of the woods was like a shelter. There wasn't a person in sight, I stood still for a moment and looked around, and the autumnal forlornness of the landscape muted my sadness. The skies were overcast, patches of grey, darkening clouds scudded overhead and showers fell on the earth here and there. And the earth gently took them in.

I carried on walking although heavy clods of earth weighed me down. But then I entered the woods, leaves rustled, bare shrubs grazed me, I bent branches apart and suddenly, the wind died down.

Close in front of me, an animal sprang up noiselessly; it was a large, grey-brown hare. He darted swiftly over roots, dodged down and then disappeared as fleet as an arrow into the depths of the woods. I saw his round form lying beneath the bushes and bent down and placed my hands on the nest where his fur-covered body had been. A trace of animal warmth remained that I felt with an unfamiliar tremor. I lowered my face and nestled it there, feeling a tiny breath, almost like a human breast.

I return from the fields. The earth clods stick to my shoes so I have to walk slowly like a farmer. I sometimes forget why I am here, on the run as it were, and imagine that I have already been living here for a long time. But if I truly were a farmer, I would know what crops are sown in these fields, how much is harvested and which soil is the most fertile. But I know none of these things. I sometimes think that farmers get their knowledge straight from heaven because they are pious and depend on celestial forces. I walk as an outsider across these fields, merely tolerated. Suddenly I loathe myself because I have no obligations. Here, in the countryside, I understand Gide's *Immoraliste* and I am like him, loaded with a similar guilt, at the mercy of a hostile, imaginary and futile freedom.

People have no idea what sin is.

Yes, I am ashamed of many things and I would like to ask for God's forgiveness. If only I were pious.

Six

In Marseille, I knew a girl whom they called Angelface. In truth, I barely knew her. I saw her just once, at night and she was standing in her room and must have thought we were intruders, Manuel and I. She slept at ground level in an ugly house. The village was two stations from Marseille; her mother lived there and when Angelface had seen enough of the town, bars and sailors, she went back and lived there like a well-brought up girl. That's probably why people called her Angelface.

But we added, 'or the port whore of Marseille'.

Manuel and I were out driving in a Ford. We drove along the coast, it was the middle of the night and we wanted to get back to Marseille. I was hungry, so we stopped at the house where Angelface lived and woke her.

Manuel kneeled on the ground and braced his arms against the wall.

'Angelface!' he shouted.

No one answered. Then she crossed the room: we couldn't see anything except her white shadow gliding towards the window. And then she pressed her pale face against the dense netting that protected the window from mosquitoes. I couldn't make out her features but my knees gave way slightly.

'It's me,' said Manuel.

'Who's with you?' asked Angelface.

'My friend,' said Manuel.

'How old is he?' asked Angelface.

'Twenty,' said Manuel. 'And we'd like something to eat.'

'I can't let you in,' said Angelface. 'My mother wakes very easily. But I'll butter you some bread.'

I went back to the car and waited for Manuel. Then he brought the sandwiches and we drove on.

'Are you in love with Angelface?' asked Manuel. And then, coldly: 'It's not very original to be in love with her.'

That was half a year ago.

Manuel and I never write to one another. But through a friend, he let me know that Angelface had shot herself.

And now I think: how unoriginal it is to love Sibylle. I don't see how anyone can resist her.——

Seven

I worked very regularly before I knew Sibylle. I got up at seven o'clock and if I had no lectures to attend, I would go to the main library at half past eight. In the morning, there were many seats empty; I would quickly find my books and start reading. The reading room is crescent-shaped and dimly lit, and the desks are arranged in a semicircle as if surrounding a speaker. I always imagined that there, at the centre of the room, a speaker should stand, a powerful man, whom we could not help gazing towards and who would reassure us with his presence.

My seat was on the left-hand side near the windows that were draped in thick curtains. They were only drawn back on bright afternoons; then the sun would filter into the room and slide lingeringly and colourlessly across the floor. I couldn't see out but the noise from the street would rise up, enticing me. I would imagine the cars below driving back and forth and overtaking each other, people rushing into restaurants, reading newspapers and feeling snug, and I would pack up my books and leave.

No one would take any notice: everyone was alone here and paid no attention to the others.

I would then go to a restaurant and order something to eat. And nearly always, I would be very hungry.

Eight

But all that soon ended. And then I started spending all day in a state of nearly unbearable restlessness.

It was only when evening began that I could comfort myself; the lamps were lit and now, Sibylle would be waking up.

The thought of her name sent a bittersweet thrill through me. I would leave the library, go home, take a bath and change. I would normally eat dinner at the house of some friends. I took part in their conversations; they were educated, refined people, and the evenings passed quickly and animatedly. I concealed my impatience but whenever I glanced at my watch, it was only ever nine o'clock. I conversed mostly with the hostess, a woman whom I was very fond of and who knew my mother.

But quite suddenly one evening, everything changed. I seem to remember we were talking about the Kingdom of Germany in the Middle Ages, and about the symbolic significance of a name that provided so little reality. But all at once, I heard my own voice speaking as if coming from a stranger: a great flush came over me, I whispered Sibylle's name aloud without meaning to, saw her eternally pale face appear behind the window, ran to the window and tore back the curtains.

Everyone gaped in astonishment. What had happened?

Nothing: Sibylle's face. What did *they* understand? An endless chasm opened up between us, strangers stared at me, the earth caved in between us, the lights dulled, the conversation no longer reached my ears, then everyone vanished and I could do nothing to stop them—

I remembered at the Bayreuth Festival often seeing a special kind of scene change: as the music played on, the curtains remained open but, close by the stage front, mist rose up, diffused by coloured lights, then it grew dense, flowed together in whitish streams and formed walls that became ever more impenetrable behind which the scenery sank imperceptibly. Then all was still: the mist dispersed, the stage reappeared and a new landscape emerged, gently tinged with a new light—

I was being asked something and I answered but I have no idea if I gave a sensible answer.

I stood up and made my lonely way to the hostess, who smilingly offered me her hand.

Out on the street, I exhaled. I had escaped from danger. No one had noticed me running away.

That's how it was. I had got away, the chasm had opened up in front of me, irresistibly drawn, I had stretched out my arms and plummeted into it.

A boy skulked over to me, his head bowed, then he shot me a distrustful, questioning look.

'Are you going to leave your car here?' he asked. 'Should I look after it for you?'

I nodded.

'So you already know my car?' I asked.

I looked at my watch.

'Eleven o'clock,' said the boy. 'Eleven o'clock,' I said happily. And I hurried back to the car. As I pulled my keys out of my pocket and thought about how to get to the Walltheater, I suddenly had to catch my breath and lean my hand on the hood. The boy looked at me, frowning.

I screamed at him, 'Get in!' and unlocked the door.

Then I gripped the boy by the shoulders, pulled him roughly to me and at the same time started up the motor with my left hand.

He remained doggedly silent and stared at me in wordless resignation.

Nine

Do I often think of Sibylle?

I'd say that I don't know. I don't think about her but I haven't forgotten her for a minute. It's as if I'd never lived without her. Nothing holds us together but I am steeped in her presence. I sometimes remembered the scent of her skin or breath and it would feel as if she was still holding me in her arms while dancing or sitting next to me and I would only have to reach out my hand to touch her. But what is supposed to hold us together— these long evenings, these long nights, these farewells at her door in the dawn light, these endless periods of lone-liness?

Ten

It is not yet late but darkness has fallen over the hills like a curtain. When I think of the city, it is as if I lived there without an inkling of the world; I don't know how I could bear the confinement, the ghastly monotony of the walls, the foreboding silence of the buildings and the desolation of the streets. I would sleep but no dreams came to comfort me and when I awoke, I was tired. Then I would sit at my desk and it would grow dark again, and the headlights of cars would glide up and down my window. —The nights would always get very late. Sometimes, dawn was breaking as I drove home. At first it was dark and the headlights glittered on the black asphalt. Then the lights gradually grew pale, the streets brightened and their gleam faded. The sky between the trees in the Tiergarten was streaked with grey; sack-shaped clouds, veils and wedges drove themselves into the softening blackness, tree trunks emerged silvery, and between their branches the dawn light danced in waves.

I longed for a glimpse of the sun that was now rising somewhere, incandescent. But in the city, it was not visible. A red glint in the sky was where the East lay. Everything remained quiet.

I stopped in front of the building where my rooms were. A gentle wind buffeted me and refreshed my face. It was the morning wind. Soon it would be lost in the hubbub of the city, smothered by its pace. I went into the house, took the lift to the second floor and unlocked my apartment door. Hardly taking the time to undress, I sank into sleep.

Eleven

Today I am impatient and hurry home as if someone might be waiting for me. Yet this is impossible as no one knows where I am staying and not even a letter can reach me. I will force myself to slow down. I have taken on so much blind haste. For weeks, the city has infiltrated me from all sides, the sky has been overcast, the silence broken. But here the skies are endless and when I sit upon a knoll or lean against a tree trunk, I hear nothing but the murmurs of the wind.

I can't ever imagine spring in this mournful region, or the abundant colours of summer. Sometimes as I lie stretched out in bed, I compel myself to imagine such things and from the darkness, the sight of a field rippling in the wind gradually grows in my mind's eye: row upon row of golden stalks, an infinite number of yellow stalks joining together and moving apart in a surging mass, a moving carpet over the brown earth; in the distance, an alley is opened up by the broad strides of reapers up to their knees in the crunching yellowness, and sheaves rustle as they sink left and right to the ground. Following the men, the women come laughing and glistening from the sun and sweat, giving off a musky smell. Their bare arms grasp the falling sheaves and arrange them in tidy bundles. Under their drawn-up skirts, you can see their powerful knees.

Yes, that's how summer was—

The sky is shot through with bright rays and dazzles your eyes. The brilliance is too much to bear; you have to lower your eyes or throw yourself into the grass: it is radiantly fresh and lies gently and moistly against your glowing skin.

Or it was spring. And the skies ascended, becoming ever more diaphanous, a captivating, pastel-coloured airiness; mild winds rose, clouds scudded in the lofty space above, the sparsely leaved trees tilted their tops, straightening up then giving in to gentle quivering, the grasses, depleted and faded under the piles of snow, loosening, struggling upwards and gleaming. If you stood on the edge of the field, you would be stirred by this lushness: all around, the countryside was bathed in fresh moisture, pastel colours from lightest green to the white of the clouds; untouched blue, the light matte brown of animal skins, iridescent grey, the silver of tree bark, reddish cracks in the earth, hazelnut branches, leftovers of faded leaves, yellow primroses surfacing in brownish boglands, the black earth of garden beds veiled in grey and then the deeply furrowed, steaming clods.

You would go and tilt your face towards these luxuriant sensations, breathing in the lightly warmed air, feeling, as you strode, a shout for joy welling up; you would lift your hands to your breast and see the muted, silver line of the horizon in the distance, make out hills, streets, barely thawed, gurgling water, bridges over gorges and steep mountain peaks that rose into the surging blue, vaulted sky.

I open my eyes. The room is badly lit but now it is warm; the white stove crackles as if fir branches were burning. When I go into the woods tomorrow, I will bring back a few sticks and hold them in the flames so that they give off the scent of Christmas. It will make me homesick.

I sit up in bed. Perhaps I am feeling better. But the room lurches before my eyes and I fall back on my pillows. I ought be quite discouraged but perhaps I am too weak to feel anything. The room is so ugly. Oh, if only Willy were here! I'd like to know who slept in this rotten bed before me.

There are two beds here but I am all alone.

I rest the writing pad on my knees and the letters swim before my eyes.

Soon I will be too tired to write any more and I haven't started on my theme yet—because I do have a theme. I want to set down the story of a love affair but I keep getting distracted and only talking about myself. It's probably because I am ill. I can't make myself do anything. And I'm still caught up in the subject of my work; I got lost in wayward places, and now I want to return to life. I want to get back to a daily routine of eating, drinking and sleeping well.

That's why I went away but at that point, I ought not to have become ill: because now, more than ever, I'll be thrown back to thinking about the queerest situations. And I am writing again. I haven't stopped all these weeks in fact; I was living my life as if contemplating my every move and it didn't do me any good. I know nothing about Sibylle, I have failed to contemplate her. Or Willy . . .

But is it possible to contemplate Sibylle?

Can I contemplate the weapon that injured me?

('You were a weapon, Sibylle, but in whose hands?')

Twelve

Today the hunt begins. I come downstairs, it is shortly before one o'clock; the hotelkeeper standing in the hallway, greets me and says, 'The hunt is open.' At first, I don't understand what he means. It sounds like: 'The window is open,' and I say, 'Ah, that's good,' and continue on my way. But the hotelkeeper follows me and sits down at my table. 'Tomorrow, there'll be haunch of venison,' he says. 'But you're not a keen hunter, then?'

'No,' I say. And still he goes on to tell me how much game there is in these woods, how much was shot last year and what sorts of prices it can fetch on the market. He uses several specialist terms that I don't always understand although I knew them at one time. But these words have never entered my mind again. I'm sure entire worlds of language get lost in this way, things that were once commonplace and self-evident and part of one's life. It's the same with names.

I listen to the hotelkeeper and ask who is going on the hunt. He says the landowners from around here. They meet and ride with their hunting rifles and their light-footed horses into the woods. They have special picnic spots, usually sheltered glades, or little meadows surrounded by bushes and high trees. It's a very jolly occasion. Even the ladies join the hunt and guide the coachmen who provide baskets of provisions from carriages. The hotelkeeper says that before the war, the hunts were lavish and elegant: nearly every evening there was a large dinner at his hotel. That, of course, has all changed now. These days, people have to tighten their belts—

After eating, I go out and walk slowly through the little town. I feel better today, in fact, I could try to go for a walk, it would do me no harm. But before I do, I'd like to take coffee somewhere.

I enter the patisserie where, a few days ago, I wrote the first pages of these notes. The puppy is no longer there. The owner is a little excited; it must be due to the hunt.

I order coffee. At the window, two tables from mine, three gentlemen sit in thick grey topcoats with fur collars. These topcoats are made of military material and have green cuffs. The three gentlemen are talking about the hunt. I hear the same specialist terms and, again, they seem familiar to me. We learned how to shoot at school and my father sometimes practised with me during the holidays. But it never interested me especially and it's been a long time since I held a weapon in my hands. It makes no difference to me, I loathe hunting. I can't understand how people can love animals and hunt at the same time.

Sibylle once said to me that she'd hold it against me if I'd ever killed an animal. I told her I'd never done such a thing. But she didn't believe me. When it comes down to it, I believe that Sibylle is more capable of killing than I am. She has a very female cruelty: that was often said to warn me. It was only unbearable at first. I didn't mean much more to her than Willy.

Willy let her tell him what to do. She was ruthless towards him: and this, even though he was otherwise quite conceited. I thought I was the one who'd discovered Willy. I was mistaken. Sibylle had already known him for years and he'd only made friends with me because he noticed I was interested in Sibylle. But that's an ill-chosen word: I was only interested in myself, and in such a skilful way that I considered myself free, even after I'd been living in a very strange, foreign, hermetic world for a long time. I believe we can only take control of situations once we're no longer personally involved in them. If I hadn't loved Sibylle so much perhaps I could have meant something to her. I believe that. But, as it was, I couldn't mean anything to her, quite simply because I was too deeply in love with her. Soon I shall go home. I don't have the inclination to think of all the mistakes I've made. Most of them were inevitable and the advice from my friends didn't help me at all.

Now I have constant headaches and I think I am feverish again every evening. But I'll be patient. I could perhaps go into the woods but the hunters are out there now and I don't want to run into them. The three gentlemen at the neighbouring table have drunk their wine and are leaving. I watch them go although they do not interest me in the slightest. Then I leave too.

It's already dark outside. I am very happy that the days are so short and pass so quickly. But why should it make me happy? I have no reason to count the days. I have no goal before me.

I walk slowly through the little town. It's actually just one street called Hauptstrasse and it's illuminated. People are gathered in front of a shop, I hear a loudspeaker from afar announcing the weather. Then the daily news follows, and a waltz begins . . .

A dog stands between the men's legs and yaps at the invisible loudspeaker. A worker gives the dog a kick. Sibylle would certainly have said something to him. She doesn't approve of animals being maltreated. Once—it was at the beginning of our acquaintance—she shouted at an old man who was dragging his dog along behind him. It was late at night and the dog was half-starved. It wasn't wearing a collar, the man had just tied a string around its neck and with it, he was tugging the animal forwards and cursing.

I was walking behind Sibylle and almost stumbled over the dog. I simply didn't see it because I was so terribly tired. It had all just begun back then: Sibylle would stay after her performance in the Walltheater until three o'clock in the morning. She would arrive at eleven but I wouldn't be able to see her then because she would be getting ready in her dressing room. It would take her a long time. Later, I would sometimes go in to her, she didn't seem to mind. The old dressing-room woman would pull a chair up for me and I would sit so that I could see Sibylle in front of the mirror as I leaned my back against the wall. Afterwards, between twelve and one o'clock, Sibylle would sing. She wore a rust-brown dress and looked absolutely beautiful, like a Gothic angel except a trace more boyish because of her narrow hips. Singing wasn't important to her; she took her bows at the end like all other singers and, in general, behaved with decorum. Only she didn't hold the curtain with one hand or pull it to one side but stood there instead, quite detached, waiting for it all to be over.

Once she'd finished, she'd come over to my table and order drinks. She would stay until three o'clock. I would too because I didn't want to part from her. Then we would leave, almost always alone, and outside, Willy would appear and ask if he should order a car. But my car was mostly parked there or we would take a little walk. Willy would follow at a distance and when we ate, he would wait outside with the drivers. It was only when he noticed that I accompanied Sibylle to her front door that he stayed away. Sibylle didn't appear to notice any of this and it was all the same to me.

That very night, I was so tired that for the first time I couldn't hide it. I stopped talking altogether and couldn't eat either. Sibylle asked, 'How's your work getting on?' I remember her words exactly because I was so astonished that she'd asked about it. But I said nothing. 'I think you need to get more sleep,' she said and laid her hand on my arm. Otherwise she said nothing. And later, on the street, I stumbled over the dog. She stopped instantly and scolded the old man, telling him he should let go of the string. 'Can't you see the dog can't walk a step further?' she said and I had never heard her speak so sharply. The man cursed terribly and I thought there would be a scene. I wanted to put myself between Sibylle and the man but she sent me back to the bar—we had only walked a few paces—and said I should fetch some milk. I left and ran into Willy. He was huddled among a group of young men at the bar. When I came in, he slid off his chair and asked if Sibylle had forgotten something. Then he fetched the milk and came with me. Sibylle was standing, still bent over the dog and seemed to be explaining to the old man how to look after the animal. He was scolding in a low voice that the dog had to come home and Sibylle said that the dog would go of its own accord once it had drunk the milk. But it took quite a long time before the dog started drinking. Clearly, it was frightened. Afterwards, it trotted docilely after the old man.

In the meantime, Willy had fetched a car. Sibylle said that she was very tired and asked if I wanted to drive with them. But it wasn't worth it and I said goodbye to Sibylle, watching as they drove away. I had an empty feeling in my stomach and felt quite light-headed.

Willy didn't say goodbye: he was sitting up front next to the driver, looking very pleased with himself. I don't think he minded staying up all night.

Thirteen

Then I met Erik. He was from Sweden and was related to Magnus but I didn't know that; I met him in the Walltheater bar and Sibylle introduced us. He asked if I skied. As soon as there was snow, he said, he would be going to Switzerland to ski for three months. He had a wife and two children whose pictures he carried around in his wallet. He showed me them when he took out his wallet to pay. He also had a profession but he didn't seem to take it seriously and never mentioned it. Besides this, Sibylle seemed to have known him for a long time. I liked him a lot. He drank one whisky in the time it took me to drink three cognacs and a whisky; he noticed this and said that surely it wasn't good for me. At that, Sibylle laid a hand on his shoulder and said 'Don't worry, you can leave that to me.'

I found it a strange thing for her to say and didn't quite dare look at him. He left soon afterwards. Sibylle accompanied him out but then returned, ordered drinks and didn't so much as look at me. When her coat was fetched, I paid and left with her. That night, there was no dog on the street. Willy was standing near the door as we got in the car. Sibylle tilted the seat forwards and asked if he wanted to come with us. He looked at me and said, using the *Sie* form, 'You've forgotten to turn on the headlights.' I replied, 'Why are you saying *Sie* to me?' Sibylle looked straight ahead and told me which way to drive. It was about four o'clock in the morning, it was misty and the streets were very wet and slippery. I drove slowly but Sibylle was terribly impatient and stamped her foot from time to time. I stepped on the accelerator and clenched my teeth. I wasn't driving very carefully and all of a sudden, a huge fallen tree loomed up ahead of us. It was lying right at the fork of two roads and looked like a rough-skinned colossus in the damp, mist-shrouded darkness. I don't remember exactly how I managed to drive past it. Sibylle suddenly said, 'Turn right,' in her characteristically low, soothing voice and then we were already driving along the next street.

We drove for a very long time. Finally, I asked Sibylle where she wanted to go. 'Where?' she asked. 'I don't know. Why do we need to know?' I drove to a service station—it was closed—then I asked a driver on the next corner where there was a night service station. It was quite a long way away and when we got there, I had no water left in the radiator.

'So you like Erik?' asked Sibylle.

'He's very clever.'

I glanced at the dashboard and slowed down.

'This car's going to rack and ruin the way it's being treated,' I said. It was an exaggeration but I was angry and sad, and I love the car. I paid a third of it with my earnings, and my father paid for the other two thirds before he left for Russia for big oil drillings.

At last, we reached the service station.

It was an Olex pump and the man was very friendly. I tried to unscrew the water cap. Steam rose in clouds from the radiator. The air was very cold but the metal was so hot, I couldn't touch it with my bare fingers.

When I looked up, I suddenly thought about how I was standing in the full beam of both headlamps with darkness all around. I was standing as if on a lit podium in the centre of the darkened world and all that remained, like the sea and an island, was the deadly night and us, the car, the man from the service station, me and Sibylle. The front windscreen of the car was misted over but behind it, I saw Sibylle's face emerge surreally, her eyes shimmering like pale flowers.

I no longer felt the cold. I went to pay but only had large notes; Sibylle opened the door and gave me two five-mark coins. The man said goodbye and we drove away. It was only then that I noticed Willy wasn't in the car any more.

Soon after that, we lost our bearings. The streets were empty and there was no one to ask the way. We always drove very quickly.

Then we drove over a bridge; perhaps we wouldn't have noticed it if the noise of the car hadn't suddenly changed. I pulled up on the right. The bridge wasn't lit but the headlamps illuminated a wedge of train track; in the shadows, we saw immense concrete pillars towering up, and, above them, dark ironwork, wide arches that fanned out and were supported and connected by many struts. I opened the window and leaned out. The water was rushing swiftly beneath us with great force; some light shone on its surface so that you could see the scurrying, churning waves, pummelling each other in scores of eddies. The sky arched calmly above and we hung between, barely on earth.

'Beautiful,' I said.

'Yes,' said Sibylle.

'What were people thinking when they built the first bridge . . .?'

'They wanted to reach the other shore. They laid a tree trunk from one bank to the other.'

'The Indians have hanging bridges. They sway as you walk over them. And they stretch over abysses.'

'But now people build incredible bridges. In New York, for example. And in Sweden, I know a concrete bridge that looks like it was cut out of glossy white paper, with lots of delicate pillars.'

'We should go visit the Indians,' I said. 'We should get hold of some money.'

'Nothing could be simpler,' Sibylle said. 'But you can't leave. They won't let you.'

'Nothing could be simpler,' I said.

Sibylle lit another cigarette. She almost always smoked while we were driving and sometimes gave me a cigarette that she first lit then pushed between my lips.

'It could cost you your career,' she said.

I've perhaps forgotten to mention that I want to become a diplomat. My father has already prepared the ground for me. It's one of his conditions that I finish my law studies and take up French and English lessons. But I'd completely neglected the language courses for weeks.

'It could cost you your career,' repeated Sibylle. The word 'career' meant nothing to me any more. It was an empty word.

'Whatever that means nowadays,' I said ill-humouredly. Magnus and I had often discussed the fact that our generation had little left except the huge benefit of friendship. By this, we meant that all the normal circumstances were missing, all the aims worth fighting for were uncertain, every kind of stability in our lives had gone. We thought that this brought us up against the ultimate meaninglessness of such goals in life; we'd lost bourgeois ambition, seen through the flimsiness of success and had got used early in life to the so-called resignation of people in their fifties. But for people in their twenties, it contained a greater cheeriness and courage, and a touch of positive self-restraint.

We thought it was very fortunate to find similarly minded friends, and to feel as close to them as brothers: to live, travel, reflect, emotionally support and love each other seemed to be our privilege. But still, I'd never given serious thought to sacrificing my career prospects. Now I imagined that I could travel with Sibylle and before me materialized images of port towns, wide rivers with bobbing boats, steppes, wandering herds of animals, aero-dromes with newly built wooden hangers, trucks on white streets and the blistering sun on covered verandas.

'What I'd like most is if we never came back,' I said. Then I noticed that Sibylle was smiling and looking straight ahead. She didn't seem to be thinking of bridges any more.

'Let's drive,' she said.

I sat up and felt for the key in the dark.

'But I can't go on any more,' I said.

I was suddenly hit by such despair that it was like someone had just woken me from an exhausted sleep.

Sibylle looked at me in silence.

'I can't go on any more,' I repeated. And then the night began to spin vertiginously around us. I pressed my hand to my eyes: coloured spots came drifting through the darkness, drew nearer to my face, grew big, flared and exploded. Nausea rose chokingly in my throat. I turned my head as if I could escape myself.

Sibylle turned abruptly to me and put her hands on my face. Her hands were cool. It was if someone had laid my head on fresh linen.

After a while, she gave me something to drink from a small bottle that she carried with her. It tasted very strong and I drank it reluctantly. She had laid my head on her shoulder and I felt better. Occasionally her breath caressed me as if we were dancing together and from time to time she pressed her chin and her cheek against my forehead for a moment.

I started up the engine and we drove. It was an unspeakable strain for me to drive in a straight line. I thought at any moment that I wouldn't be able to keep hold of the wheel. The street moved up and down in heavy swells: trees, lanterns, even the straight line of the pavement came into sight at the last moment. Everything seemed to lurch into my line of vision at the same time, bewildering me. Sibylle touched my shoulder with her left hand. That calmed me. Sometimes she gripped me harder. I must have been driving very slowly because, on a sudden impulse, she pushed my foot off the pedal and accelerated herself: it was a dangerous way of driving. After a short time, I stopped, opened the door and said, 'Now you can drive.'

She seemed a little taken aback but she just said, 'If you wish . . .' then remained sitting there for a few seconds, looking at me. Then we changed places. I didn't even know if she knew how to drive but I was so exhausted by then that I didn't care.

She didn't start up the engine straight away so I put the car in gear and shifted for her until we were in third, then I leaned back and looked out through the slightly fogged window. We were on Heerstrasse, somewhere far outside the city. We drove very fast. At times, the car veered towards the side of the road as if drawn by a magnet. That was very dangerous, and when we came close to the kerb or another barrier, I often had to wrench the steering wheel the other way at the last minute.

It was getting light by now. A thin layer of mist hung in the woods just a metre or so above the ground, shrouding the trunks of the spruce trees. When I turned my head, I saw a weak tinge of crimson in the sky. Otherwise, everything was ice-grey, cold and still. We were approaching the city and I sat down at the wheel again. Sibylle's face had changed: she seemed very tired but wasn't as pale as usual and her eyes were brighter. As she got out at her front door, she pressed my hand to her cheek and said I must promise to drive home carefully and not get up before midday. I drove to my apartment and parked the car on the street. It was daylight now. I felt quite good and went up to the second floor without using the lift. In the bedroom, the maid had drawn the curtains: it was dark and I laid myself on the bed straight away. But I couldn't sleep. I thought of the drive and how insanely dangerous it had been. Sibylle had driven so fast that we probably would have rolled over if we'd hit the kerb. But it wasn't that. There was something much worse: I realized that I hadn't cared if we'd met with an accident. Sibylle had asked me: 'Were you afraid?' And I'd said no, and I was being honest. I was too tired to be afraid. I'd thought, if she wants to smash our skulls, let her try.

And then, crouching on my bed, I still didn't care; I couldn't feel any horror at the thought that I might have died. But as I realized this, a kind of hopelessness seized me. I flung myself down and began to cry uncontrollably, fearing for my life for the first time.

Fourteen

The next day, I slept in until noon. Once, at around eleven, the maid came in and put some coffee on a low table near my bed. She asked if she should bring me something to eat but I told her I felt very unwell and would like most of all to sleep some more. When I got up two hours later, I felt sick. I had to lie down again and was quite drenched in sweat. I lay there without moving until the telephone rang next door. It was Erik. He asked if I wanted to have breakfast with him; he would pick me up in half an hour. 'You're giving me reason to worry,' he said.

I had a bath and got dressed. All the time, I still felt light-headed as I did most mornings. I thought I eventually might get used to this state.

Erik arrived very punctually. First he glanced at my books and then stood in front of my desk. 'Do you work a lot?' he asked. 'You're still studying, how very lucky.' I didn't know how to reply. 'I've always been an explorer,' said Erik. 'At your age, I think I was an intellectual explorer.'

Above the desk hung a large photograph of Sibylle. She was wearing short trousers and an open-neck shirt with a bold check pattern. Her pale face was exaggeratedly lit, making it almost look like a mask. But you could see the slightly subdued, characteristic glint in her eyes as if it had penetrated through many layers of darkness. 'She has wonderful eyes,' said Erik. 'I saw Magnus yesterday. Do you know what he says about you? But come, get your coat; we want to go. Well—he says there's nothing that can be done to help you. You're too young to take such emotional turmoil. That's right, you're susceptible and a slave to desire, like a schoolboy. It wasn't a very kind way of putting it. But I know that Magnus is very fond of you and it pains him to have to lose respect for you. It was Strindberg who once wrote somewhere: "Mankind is to be pitied."'

The conversation made me very uncomfortable. When you're suffering, it's hard to bear someone not taking your anguish seriously.

'Magnus seems to know all about it,' I said.

'No,' said Erik. He parked in front of the Atelier restaurant and a *Schupo* told him to park closer to the kerb. He did so and I waited for him. I was freezing. Then we went in and Erik carefully ordered our food. He treated me like a little child. I can still remember all the details of that meal because it was the first time in a while that I'd eaten at a table that was properly laid and where the food was hot and delicious. While eating, we spoke. It was a very wary conversation, a conversation between covert opponents. Suddenly I asked:

'Do you love Sibylle then?'

He said nothing and seemed surprised. Very slowly, he replied:

'Two years ago, every evening I went to an awful cabaret in Brussels. Sibylle was on stage there. Why do you think I go to the Walltheater these days?'

I didn't know him well at all but I was afraid he might regard me as a rival. And at that moment, I needed a friend. I was very much on my own.

'Should I leave?' Erik asked. 'Perhaps you'd like me to disappear?'

'No,' I said, 'That wouldn't help'.

I knew quite well that if Erik went away, it wouldn't help things between Sibylle and I. And we hadn't even asked her what she thought.

'People say that Sibylle is a cold woman,' said Erik. 'Dear boy, you aren't eating. Let's change the subject.'

'Sibylle has been the only thing on my mind for weeks,' I said. Erik pushed a dish towards me and put a helping on my plate.

'I think she's been through a lot,' he said. 'She's certainly ruined a few people. And it's not only bad sorts she has on her conscience.'

'Yesterday I suddenly felt afraid,' I said.

Outside the sun was shining. It wasn't coming in directly but some rays filtered through the curtains and spread a gentle, deep-toned warmth on the brick walls. A woman was walking through the restaurant and for the length of a second, the barely visible sunrays fell on her face; it shone and her blonde hair looked for that same second like liquid gold.

My hands were cold although the restaurant was well heated.

'They always said something bad would happen to me.' I said 'But I never believed it. My teachers said that I would come to a sticky end.'

'Yes, well, one always imagines things will be different from how they turn out.'

'I'm not jealous,' I said. I hoped very much that Erik would see that we were natural allies. Why should I be jealous if he loved Sibylle or even if Sibylle loved him? In the end, we would all share the same language. I felt some comfort in that.

Fifteen

The echo of shots rings out from the woods and around the little town, unsettling the calm. Early this morning, I went to the palace gardens, and the old palace walls were trickling with damp. The palace is beautiful, although it's hard to make out any kind of style: princes through the ages have lived here and built, demolished or extended according to their needs. A few of the windows on the upper floors of the round turrets are little more than arrow slits but the numerous windows in the long main building are high and decorated with late baroque ornamentation. The porter lives in a room with a simple stucco ceiling and a floor made of white-scrubbed pinewood. The palace courtyard is paved and so large that a car could easily turn in it. At the front towards the park and the water, both side wings are joined by a straight colonnade. The columns are pale pink, yellow or white in the shifting light and I always feel like leaning against one of them to look down at the park. At the moment, the view is rather bleak: the trees are leafless, and the yellow and rust-brown foliage lies on the surface of the water. Today the branches were coated in thick, lush dew and looked almost frosted. I would like to stay outside all day. My throat feels dry although I drink a lot. I had a bad night's sleep.

I leave. I don't want to walk through the woods as usual but take the path instead that leads past the church then inconspicuously leaves the town and leads into sandy, flat, scattered hills. I walk quite fast at first. I'm glad to get away from the woods, from the cushioned mossy ground, the rabbit hollows, the trickling sound of pine needles. From warm animal nests.

Here there is only bare expanse, a great rolling sea of hills. The ground has soaked up a lot of moisture over the past weeks. On the right, the hills have been sliced open: work is being done in the sand pits, a mechanical digger makes a din, the thin, clean air trembles from the noise and a black crane towers overhead. I go to the edge of the pit and watch the workers. They are serious, self-possessed, formidable men. They've been hard at it since early this morning and they eat their lunch outdoors, and in the evening they'll walk unfalteringly the long way back to the town.

I walk on and after I've been going for over an hour, I come to a village. The street is cobblestoned down the middle, and on either side stand low, grey houses with roofs that don't reach over the walls: they don't even provide shelter from the rain. I continue to the local tavern, and take a seat inside. It's roomy, low and half-lit. The walls are blackened. The furniture is heavy and rough, and the wood is light-coloured and has a patina. Over the bar hangs a picture of Bismarck framed in an oak wreath.

The innkeeper doesn't have any writing paper so I first go into the centre of the village and find a shop where I also buy ink and a fountain pen. Then I return to the tavern, order red wine and set the paper out next to me. I can't write just yet, the walk has tired me.

And then I write after all. Dear God, it's already become a habit of mine and I will write a whole book, more or less by accident . . . I'll send the book to Sibylle, she'll read it and say if she thinks it's good or not. If she thinks it's good, I'll have it published—

No.

I don't have the ambition for that.

People always said that, because of Sibylle, I betrayed all my good qualities.

And they had high hopes of me once. But everyone eventually agreed with Magnus—even I had to admit it in the end and it made me very sad. Then they said it was good that I was facing the truth and what did I hope to gain from Sibylle. Of course, I didn't hope to gain anything from her and if they reproached me that it was impossible to live with a woman like Sibylle, I knew better than they did why that was. They all imagined that Sibylle was the ideal lover: but only I knew that she wasn't interested, not even if I'd had money, not even if I were ten years older and my own master. They all thought that Sibylle was deceiving me and didn't send me away because she was manipulative. They couldn't imagine that a woman like Sibylle could live without a lover. But to me, Sibylle sometimes seemed so strangely preoccupied that I felt very far from her intimacy. I knew that she was lying to me, or at least that she was concealing something important, perhaps the most important thing in her life. I once told her this. It was late at night and we were having a drink in a cellar bar in Kantstrasse. She was being unkind to me and this made me morose, so I asked her. Without a pause, she shot back that she wouldn't sacrifice even a minute of her sleep if she weren't fond of me. At that moment, I realized that *I* was sacrificing my sleep for *her* and besides, that I loved her for it in the same way that one might hate someone else. Or perhaps I had grown to hate her too in the meantime. But I might just as well have hated myself.

I was told a great many things about Sibylle—that she'd lived with a driver, for instance, and later with an art dealer: the driver was in prison and the art dealer had shot himself.

That was nonsense, of course, fabrication and gossip. But on the other hand, it could equally have been true. In the end, one can only die for Sibylle. To live for her, my friends say, is degrading.

But they did not understand her in the least. They made their lives so very simple: otherwise, existence would have been too difficult to bear. Because everything is so horribly shackled together, every action has a thousand repercussions, the responsibility is enormous and no judgement is right or fair. And still, we have to live on . . .

Sixteen

I started seeing Erik every day and we became good friends. We ate together, he picked me up from home, sometimes he woke me and it was already two o'clock in the afternoon, and when I got up I felt sick. He said he wanted to send me to the doctor but he realized that there was no point.

'You must really enjoy being ill and not being able to work any more,' he said. But I hated it: it was simply that I couldn't do anything about it or find a way out. I had become so despondent that I didn't dare think about something. I'd never believed that something seriously bad could happen to me: I still didn't believe it, but I'd become fearful and when I came home and it was dark, or it was just getting light on the streets, I sometimes thought that I would never find my way again. I didn't breathe a word of this to anyone, not even Erik. He probably guessed, he was very concerned about me.

'Sibylle's probably going to travel with me,' he said one day. 'She could go on a trip with you too if you had money, but I think she's more likely to come with me.'

I nodded in approval. When Erik wanted to smoke, I fetched cigarettes from the living room and offered him one. They were in a box of inlaid wood that I'd bought in Milan. I'd been there with Magnus and his sister Edith and two other girls. They were very pretty and we'd spent half our summer holidays with them in Italy. All five of us became very good friends and in actual fact, that had only been a few months ago. When I held the box in my hand, I suddenly remembered all this quite clearly: the shop had been in a small, dark alleyway near the cathedral; the cathedral square had stood white and dazzling in the sun; on the steps in front of the entrances, sleeping beggars had lain, with children darting in between them. Now and then, the dark curtain in front of the door would be pulled aside and a priest would come quickly down the steps to the square below. He would be wearing a claret-coloured sash over his black gown. We wandered around the city and drank a lot until we drove home in the evenings on the main highway to our house in the middle of the countryside amid mulberry trees. Now I held the box from Milan in my hand: it was in Berlin, my friends were far away, and I'd forgotten about them.

'Erik,' I said, 'Can you imagine Sibylle being dead?'

'Oh yes,' he said.

'Or not knowing her? Or that she was made up? Can you imagine living without her and being free?'

'Dear boy, you really ought to free yourself.'

'Then I wouldn't see her any more,' I said. 'That's simply impossible, I can't give her up. But when I think that once—'

It was astounding: it was just a memory but it jolted me quite suddenly into realizing that I'd once been very cheerful and quite without a care and since then, I'd carried Sibylle inside me like an ominous dream—

Sibylle was still performing on stage and wore a different dress that I liked even more than the first. It had a plunged, round neckline, and it fitted so tightly over her hips that the outline of her slender body could be clearly seen through it. Her hair was somewhat straighter, and her bare temples stood out. They were white and translucent, her hands were translucent, her face shimmered palely and under her eyes were blue shadows.

Seventeen

Just when I was on best terms with Erik, he left. He said he had business to do and would return in eight days. On the first day, I went very late to the theatre and resolved not to wait for Sibylle.

There were a great many people and it was a struggle to get to my usual seat.

On stage, Fred and Ingo were doing a dance number. They'd been doing the same set for three months but that was the case everywhere, and they were successful.

To them, it was of no importance at all what they did: they learned the dance moves and they practiced diligently. The whole show was just a run-through of their agility, their hard work and their youthfulness. I found the two of them dull but I appreciated that they were innocent and charming, and that's what people wanted to see. And as I said, it was the same everywhere: in the evening, the city was full of glittering, splendidly furnished halls where handsome young people showed themselves off; everything was slick, dreadfully noisy and brash, and it had nothing in the least to do with art or any profound emotions. It was an awfully senseless waste of time and even the busiest of people were astoundingly short-sighted and passive. However, there was probably little sense in fighting all this when most people were not capable of making any real progress.

Yet some individuals tried to again and again and even managed to accomplish great deeds; but these were simply laid aside, unused, and a continually declining number of people took notice of them. It was just the same with the findings of philosophers: there were scholars who explored something their whole life long gathering reams of material and, at the end of their life, they had achieved their goals. They thought they'd done mankind a service, and taken a further step towards greater knowledge. They knew that this knowledge would ultimately lead to knowledge of God. But then the books lay idle in libraries and no one read them because no one had time for such things apart from a few specialists in their field. And even *they* hardly had time to read all the essentials of a life's work. And how many of these thoughts were in the end essential, and what convoluted routes did it take to find them?—

When Fred and Ingo had finished dancing, I ordered a cognac. The waiter told me that Sibylle had already been on stage and was sure to come soon. Only then did I notice that the people on the table next to mine were looking at me and obviously expecting me to greet them. I did so because there was a lady among them. She was sitting with her back to me but she turned and smiled and asked if I would care to join her table. 'You look so troubled,' she said. I told her I was in very good spirits, blushing as I said it because she was so beautiful and because I really didn't know her name. Her companion was elegant and bald and had dull, shifty eyes. She had radiant eyes and a candid, gently seductive, intense expression.

She talked about many people I used to see at one time or who were acquaintances of my parents. I managed to compose myself and we conversed amiably. Occasionally, she said something surprising that I found myself unable to answer. Then she went silent and her eyes became even more expressive.

'I'd like to know where you were last night,' she said. 'I'd like to know where you spend your other life.'

'I'd prefer you not to know,' I said. It was a clumsy, defiant answer, and I blushed again.

She laughed and her companion laughed too. He never said anything himself but only agreed with everything afterwards, as if confirming what she'd said. Then she would look over at him in a friendly way, and seemed to be fond of him. I was astonished when I heard that he was her husband. He seemed so insignificant. When Sibylle arrived, I stood up, said goodbye and we both sat down at my table.

A few days later, I was invited by Frau von Niehoff to dinner. She'd completely slipped my mind. When I saw her again, I was surprised to see that she was even more beautiful than I'd remembered. I arrived a little early; her little girl was still up and having supper on a blue tray. She was a very pretty girl of about five years of age and I fell in love with her immediately. She had light blond hair, was very gentle and had the same name as her mother: Irmgard.

When we were alone, Frau von Niehoff said she thought I seemed ill and it would be better if I went home straight away. I didn't feel any worse than usual. 'But you can't go about looking like that,' she said. 'I'm older than you so I have the right to scold you. And I'll look after you.'

I said 'Thank you,' and my throat felt as if it was being corded up. I thought she would then ask me about Sibylle, and whether I was having a relationship with her. And I felt desperate at the thought that I could never explain to her how things between Sibylle and I really were. She would either laugh at me or feel pity—and neither was bearable.

But she didn't ask me.

At dinner, there were two other gentlemen that I'd once met at a soirée, and a woman that Frau von Niehoff seemed to be friends with. She had a non-descript face but she was friendly and talked to me for the entire dinner.

At twelve o'clock I wanted to meet Sibylle. I said to Frau von Niehoff that I had to go. 'Is it so urgent?' she asked.

'Yes, I have a prior engagement,' I said.

'Then keep it short and come back later.' She gave me the house key so that the maid wouldn't have to come down. When her friend saw her give me the key, she

stared at Frau von Niehoff and seemed displeased but
Frau von Niehoff just gave a loud abrupt laugh before
accompanying me into the hallway. Outside she said: 'Is
there really nothing that can be done for you? Can't I do
anything?' and she brushed her hand across my forehead.
I felt something in me go weak and I quickly descended
the stairs.

Sibylle was already waiting for me.

She wanted to leave straight away so I fetched her
coat and gave the waiter a tip for keeping my table free.
We drove off and I asked if Willy had been there. I'd have
liked him to come tonight to accompany Sibylle home
later on.

But he'd been gone for a few days now and Sibylle
said that she hadn't seen him either. But she said it in
such an offhand way that I didn't believe her. I always
had the feeling that she was hiding many things from me
but it was impossible to ask her: even after several weeks,
I still didn't know her real name.

We first drove past the Memorial Church, down
Tauentzienstrasse and along Lutherstrasse. After that, I
wasn't familiar with the area any more but we drove quite
a long way and Sibylle had me wait in front of a house
with the number 34. The house had intricate balconies
and jutting cantilevers and it looked like it had been elegantly bourgeois twenty years ago. Now, however, it was
a little dilapidated. Sibylle had a key to the front door. I
waited, smoking, and while I waited, I thought of Irm-

gard von Niehoff. I took her door key out of my pocket and examined it closely.

And suddenly, I realized I was aroused, and could only think of Frau von Niehoff, and how I'd rather she were here now instead of Sibylle. I immediately felt released, and warmth and an ecstatic thrill flowed through me.

So there are other women, I thought and was captivated by the memory of Irmgard.

There are much simpler ways to be happy than I am now.

I will put Sibylle behind me.

I don't love her, I've just grown used to being near her.

It's as if she's cast a kind of spell on me.

Irmgard has black hair, a beautiful gaze and asked me if there was anything she could do for me—

'She has the most beautiful gaze,' I murmured to myself, driving all thoughts of Sibylle out of my mind.

She came back and I started up the motor.

I didn't ask what she'd done in that stranger's house. My intuition told me that she'd had important business to do, or that she was in danger in some way and would need my help. But I was accustomed to not asking questions. It was apparently none of my business.

'I'll show you which way to go,' said Sibylle, her voice drifting to my ears from far away and yet sounding unaltered.

We drove back and stopped at a corner where two taxis were parked. Their lights were off and the drivers were nowhere to be seen. In front of an ordinary little door, a man was standing who greeted Sibylle. She said to me, 'You could come in if you like. You needn't say anything but if someone talks to you, you mustn't be rude.' Then she quickly took a few banknotes out of her bag and gave them to me.

'It's better to put them in your inside pocket,' she said. And to the doorman, 'He's a friend of mine.'

He let us in. Behind the door, there were two curtains and a small bar-room that was almost completely filled by a long broad counter. A barman stood on one side and a crowd of men were standing or sitting on the other, drinking. They were mostly drivers, and not one was elegantly dressed. The others looked like small-time employees: they were wearing suits of cheap and plain blue-violet or reddish cloth, and coloured shirts with shiny silk ties.

Sibylle went past these people; some turned and greeted her with familiarity, and the man behind the bar was very courteous to her. A second room lay behind the bar: it was dimly lit and overheated by an iron stove. The room was quite barren: square tables covered in waxed tablecloths stood next to each other, three on either side. On the wall hung a printed sign with the words:

IN THE INTEREST OF OUR ESTEEMED CUSTOMERS,

WE ASK YOU TO SPEAK QUIETLY

And another:

NO RESPONSIBILITY CAN BE ACCEPTED FOR

LOST ITEMS

The walls were covered with purple wallpaper. We sat down and a waiter said that there was cold roast pork with Brussels sprouts on the menu. He was slightly deaf and Sibylle had to repeat a few times that he should bring us some beer. At last, he brought us two small glasses of dark brew.

Apart from us there was only one other couple sitting at a table in the room: the man was tall and grossly fat, and the woman had black curly hair like a Negress, and was heavily made-up. She was the only woman here besides Sibylle, but Sibylle said she was a man in drag. After we'd been sitting there for some time, one of the drivers came in and sat down at our table. He took no notice of me and spoke quietly to Sibylle. She looked rather angry and told him that she wasn't going to give him some thing or another, and when she announced loudly in her beautiful, velvety voice: 'That's completely out of the question,' he stood up, shrugged his shoulders and left.

I didn't ask any questions but I found the whole episode very unpleasant, and was glad when Sibylle called the waiter over. She looked quite exhausted. It was already half past three in the morning when we left. I was dog-tired, my thoughts turned to Frau von Niehoff and I felt unhappy. But I couldn't just abandon Sibylle.

'I'm going to take you home now,' I said and put my arm around her.

'I can't,' she said. 'I can't go home now.'

My courage failed me. The beer had drained my energy even more, now I had a headache and when I looked through the car windscreen at the street, the two rows of houses caved into one; a noise rushed in my ears and impassable obstacles blocked my path.

'Let's drive,' said Sibylle, almost pleading with me. I struck my fists on the steering wheel.

'But what's the use,' I said, 'Why can't we just sleep for once? I can't take any more.'

Sibylle was quiet for a moment, and I closed my eyes and rested my forehead on my hands.

'Of course you can,' she said. 'And it's very good for you to live against your reason for once. I'm not very easy, I know.'

There was a kind of promise in her voice. But I didn't want to hear it any more. I knew quite well that she didn't love me and it was as painful as if I'd already lost her.

I thought of Frau von Niehoff like one thinks of home. But everything was already taking a different course. And I didn't even trust myself any more.

I drove Sibylle home, and she no longer objected. As we drove, it began to rain and the car aquaplaned precariously over the asphalt.

When Sibylle got out, it had started lashing down in sheets. I accompanied her to the door, my jaws clenched, and still she said nothing. After she unlocked the door, she turned around and turned up the collar of my coat.

I went back to the car, getting soaked to the skin. I felt feverish, my jaws wouldn't loosen and I drove, without clearly thinking what I was doing, to Frau von Niehoff's apartment. There, I carefully locked the car, found the house key, and found the automatic light and safety lock to the apartment. I knew I was doing something scandalous but this knowledge didn't surface sufficiently to guide my actions. Sometimes we drive: we see a sentry standing with outstretched arms, white gloves, and still we carry on, even look the sentry in the eye; no one is prepared to believe we didn't understand what his outstretched arms meant—

I stood in a strange apartment and didn't think that I might wake a maid or blunder into someone's room. I went through the large living room, along a corridor and past two doors. At the third door, I knocked and carefully pressed down the handle. The woman who was lying in the room turned over and lit a small lamp. She looked straight at me and said quickly:

'Be quiet. You'll wake the child.'

That affected me very much. I went back through the corridor and the large room and stopped near the door to the living room. I leaned against the door and when I raised my head, I suddenly caught a glimpse of myself in a tall mirror: my wet hair was plastered against my temples, and I looked terribly pale. I sank my head again and waited. In fact, I began to weep. I was ashamed and had no resistance. I desperately hoped that the lady of the house would come, then I wished that I were outside and alone on the street.

Then she came. She turned the light on, crossed the carpet, went around the table, then stood in the doorframe and studied me. I looked at her and stopped weeping but my whole body was shaking uncontrollably.

'Come in,' said Irmgard. She led me into the living room, sat down in a large chair and I sat down opposite her.

'You have clearly gone insane,' she said.

'Yes.' I said. 'No. Not insane. Just terribly tired.'

She sat there and looked at the tips of her feet. She was wearing blue leather slippers and her feet were very white, the skin taut over her slender ankles.

'I am so sorry,' I said. 'Please, forgive me.'

And naturally, I should have got up then, I should have said goodbye and gone. But in truth, I wasn't capable of doing so. I didn't have the least shred of energy. I felt a curious mix of self-contempt, satisfaction and misery.

'I'm not normally so ill-mannered,' I said.

Irmgard leaned forward, smiled and brushed her palm several times across my eyes. I pressed my forehead to her hand.

'Perhaps you're afraid of being alone?' she asked gently. 'I suppose you'd like to spend the night here?'

'Yes,' I said.

'Well,' she said, 'You're putting me in a compromising position. Clearly you haven't thought about that. But you can sleep in my husband's bedroom.'

'Is he away?' I asked hesitatingly.

'Otherwise you'd have to sleep here on the couch,' Irmgard answered curtly, 'but you're in luck. I'll go and make some tea for you, just go and lie down in bed.'

She opened a door, turned on a light and took some pyjamas out of a cupboard.

'Here you are,' she said and left me in the room.

I stood there for a moment, steadying myself on the back panel of the bed. It was wide with blue covers, and on the bedside table there was a photograph of Irmgard. I felt very strange and thought at any moment that some glaring error would be exposed: perhaps it was not really five o'clock in the morning, and this apartment was not in Berlin on a certain street. Or perhaps I didn't know a woman called Sibylle, and had never been to a dive full of criminals; or perhaps Irmgard would never return— yes, most of all, perhaps Irmgard would never return.

Then I quickly undressed, flung myself into bed, felt how my head throbbed with pain and how the linen of the pillow was wonderfully cool and lightly scented with toilet water. I closed my eyes and waited for a woman. There is nothing more wonderful than waiting for a woman.

Eighteen

After this I became ill. But in fact I was already over the worst when I spent the night at Irmgard's. I slept for a stretch of twelve hours, then the maid came in and brought me something to eat and I thought it was breakfast but it was already five o'clock in the afternoon. I wanted to get up but then everything began to spin and my limbs felt weak. Irmgard came in, leading her little girl by the hand. I lay down again and ate, and the little girl watched me. I felt very fond of Irmgard and looked over at her from time to time but she was busy with her daughter. Later, I had a bath and dressed, feeling better; I thought it unnecessary when Irmgard ordered a driver to take me home in my car.

It was quite chilly and the car wouldn't start. We tried for a long time but then I had to take a taxi after all. The driver promised to treat my car carefully and take it to the garage. At nine o'clock, he brought me the key and shortly afterwards, Irmgard rang me up to wish me good night. I was already in bed and knew that I would stay there until the illness had passed, and I was much relieved. The maid brought the post and I told her some tale to explain why I hadn't slept there that night. Someone had rung on the telephone but I was not interested. I wasn't feverish but had a chill instead, as well as headaches and dizziness: but if I lay very still, I felt fine. Irmgard visited me the next day and in the evening she came again. She always kissed me and sat so close that I could reach out and touch her.

On the third or fourth day, Willy came. He looked very neat and tidy, and had said to the porter that he had a package for me. I started violently when he knocked at the door, although I couldn't have known who it was.

'Hello, Willy,' I said.

He sat down, a bottle of vermouth under his arm. It wasn't Cinzano or Cora but a special brand that Sibylle always ordered for me.

We drank and Willy told me that he didn't want to mind cars any more: he was going to learn a profession I said, 'If I wrote to my father, I could get you some money to do a proper apprenticeship.' But he shook his head and I realized I'd offended him.

'How is Sibylle?' I asked. I had put her photograph next to my bed, and Willy was gazing at it continuously.

'Three days ago, she had a quarrel,' he said. 'She can't bear it when that happens.'

'Three days ago I brought her home myself,' I said, adding it up.

'Yes,' he said. 'Afterwards I met her in the driver's bar—she was hungry.'

'And then?'

'She sent me away. She quarrelled with the driver. I was waiting on the street until seven o'clock. Then the driver drove us home.'

'What did she say to you?'

'Nothing. She never says anything. But she was crying when she came out on the street.'

I sat up in bed.

'She was crying?' I asked.

Willy nodded and poured vermouth into my glass.

'Drink up,' he said. He seemed to pity me.

'You must have noticed that she didn't want to be alone that night. I always see that. Then I stay even if she sends me away.'

'She didn't send me away,' I said. 'I was too tired.'

Willy didn't say any more after that.

It was about ten o'clock in the evening when he left. I fell asleep early and woke up again at about two o'clock in the morning: I'd had a dream about Sibylle. I got dressed, it was very unpleasant and I almost cried at the effort. In the garage, it was warm and stifling; my car had been washed and when I turned on the headlamps, the dark paintwork gleamed.

I drove to the Walltheater, parked the car in a side street and went in. The steward greeted me. I went to my table and saw Sibylle from afar. It was terrible, my knees were trembling and everyone was looking at me in astonishment: everyone except Sibylle. She gave me her hand and said: 'So there you are,' in a very dry, distant voice.

'I've been ill,' I said.

She laid her hand on mine.

When I ordered whisky, she said:

'Don't turn around. Herr von Niehoff is sitting behind us.'

The stage was already dark, and the guests were leaving. The manager came over to our table, greeted me and patted Sibylle on the shoulder.

'I have something for you,' he said, and pulled some photographs out of his pocket: Sibylle behind a pale veil, her features lost in reverie and her eyes shimmering from great depths like pale flowers.

'You're not to bring me home today,' she said.

We stood next to my car and Willy held open the door. Sibylle took me by the shoulders, turned me slowly around and gave me a long, searching look. Then she bent my head down a little, and pressed her forehead, temples and chin firmly and caressingly against my face.

I returned to my room, completely exhausted, at four o'clock in the morning.

Erik was sitting at my desk.

'Frau von Niehoff rang me up,' he said. 'She told me you were ill.'

'I'm feeling better,' I replied.

'I'd like to ask you something,' he said. 'But I'll have to be very indiscreet.'

'Go on,' I said.

'What's your relationship to Sibylle? And what do you think mine is? We're reasonable people after all.'

'I don't know,' I said, and suddenly as I looked at Erik, I grasped something and said, 'You got further than I did. You've known her longer and she loved you. She doesn't love me.'

'So you know that much,' he said, almost harshly.

'If I felt it was necessary, she'd sleep with me too,' I said and was deeply hurt. There was a strong animosity between us.

'You're lying,' said Erik. 'Poor boy. Irmgard von Niehoff says you cannot be helped. You simply need to be taken care of and she hasn't the time.'

'They never have time when it's necessary.'

'Don't you see, it just doesn't suit you to be a slave to a *varieté* singer,' said Erik. 'It's bad form. It's ruining you.

My God, I don't want to accuse you of anything but you're so terribly spoilt, and you could have the most wonderful time.'

'But Sibylle says I should learn for once that there are more important things besides reputation. It's a shame I'm spoilt. She says it's a pity.'

'What does she want to turn you into then? Yes, for God's sake, it *is* a pity! Don't you realize that nothing can be done for Sibylle?'

'But if one stood up for her . . .' I said. 'Perhaps she needs someone.'

Erik replied:

'We all need someone.'

He left and I was plagued by a terrible despair. On my desk lay a letter; it was an invitation for a reception with the English envoy, and Magnus had added that they'd asked for my address. I had probably not replied to earlier invitations. He wrote that I simply had to attend this reception as it was certainly my last opportunity.

I paced the room and imagined having to wear evening dress and running into thousands of acquaintances, and the idea was unbearable. Then I rang up Sibylle and her warm, drowsy voice soothed me.

'You should sleep,' she said. Her voice was barely audible.

'I'm going to sleep,' I said.

'Don't be sad,' said Sibylle. 'I'm here. I know when you need me. I'm here. Everything's fine.'

Her voice trailed off.

Perhaps she'd fallen asleep.

I undressed and was almost cheerful.

Then something in me tensed: I couldn't sleep and from time to time, a spasm passed through my body.

I'll not go to the Walltheater any more, I thought.

I won't drink any more.

But that won't help. Sibylle will simply think I'm like all the others and that I've failed.

She'll think I'm trying to make it easy for myself and I'm afraid of jeopardizing my career.

And she's right. And she's stronger than I am.

I only have the choice to endure it or to lose her.

Then I fell asleep. I can remember the dream I had in detail. It was about Sibylle. I suddenly saw her face, breathtakingly close, someone was hammering her existence home to me, someone was holding my heart and saying Sibylle's name in such a way that it stopped beating; someone lit up my mind for a few moments, liberating it from all thought and taught it to understand Sibylle. My nerves quivered like taut strings to the touch.

My sober body convulsed and I readily seized Sibylle's tender caresses.

Seconds passed—even these seconds passed. Sibylle pressed her face against my neck with her inimitable smile, and I saw her powdered, expressive, matte-shimmering eyes blanch.

Blanched, I say, as in the moment that followed, I awoke with a jolt. Everything felt very heavy, every sensation eluded me except an unbearable pain around my heart. I found myself lying prostrate and bewildered, thrown forwards with my fists balled beneath me.

Nineteen

It's time to stop. I have a long journey home. I've written for four hours and now I want to put my notes in order and go home. I'm a little disoriented. One shouldn't write—one is so easily prepared to forget experiences and belie feelings. I often think that I feel nothing and later on, I regard none of it as very important. Surely later, I will truly believe that I never loved Sibylle. No, I never loved her. It was like today, so still inside me that I could hear the wind outside. Am I too cowardly or not intent enough on returning to the past? In one's memory, even happy feelings are painful and it's preferable to gloss over them. But when I write, everything is stirred up again of its own accord; I don't even notice it, and suddenly I'm in the thick of it, agitated and distraught.

I have to keep reminding myself that I'm on my own.

The innkeeper asks me if I'm a writer. 'Yes,' I say. 'My God, yes.' Then I wish him a good evening and he opens the door for me. The way back seems shorter to me now than this morning. I will eat an early supper and go to bed. I can sleep as much as I like.

I hope there won't be any hunters around. Yesterday their singing kept me awake. They'd probably shot many animals and were proud of themselves, drinking to each another.

Ah, but what's it to me? What are other people to me?

I turn off the path and go around the small lake. Darkness is already falling and there is no one in sight. If I were a wayfarer, I could always do whatever came to mind, and I wouldn't be accountable to anyone. Not even to myself, for what am I, if not an errant soul? I cannot comprehend life, I cannot even make the simplest connections but I have to bear the consequences if I do something wrong.

Or I'd like to own a lot of land, these fields, part of these woods, the lake and park beyond. I'd live here and never leave. Then I'd be content and no one could take away what was mine, nothing could unsettle me. Land cannot be taken away.

Now I've reached the end of the lake, and opposite me is the palace and the colonnade running from wing to wing. The pillars reach high into the blue evening sky like saplings.

I'm at the water's edge and the water moves back and forth, lapping over the coarse sand. Then it flows back again, and the rest seeps in, leaving little rivulets behind that are washed over and smoothed out again. Further out, the lake looks quite still and on the far bank, the trees bow towards the water and are reflected in it. Here the bank is quite steep and there are no trees. A broad, sloping clearing has been made that continues up into the woods and at the highest point, a memorial to Frederick the Great has been erected. It is a simple large, grey stone, an obelisk, and the King erected it in honour of his loyal officers. They were renowned for their courage and loyalty, and their names have been carved into the stone. If one reads them, it sounds like a flourish of fanfares. I don't know why but there is something uplifting about reading these names. I have probably mentioned before that there have been many officers in my family. But at that moment, I wasn't thinking of them. Yet suddenly, I flush hotly, and my heart starts hammering, and I think I've stood before on this very spot. I am ashamed, I wish I had a sword; I am ashamed although I am alone and on the stone, I read the names of my ancestors.

Twenty

But now I'll continue my story and so come to the end. I'm not tired any more. I'm getting used to being alone. Everything is unreal and changed and very far removed from the usual things. I want to be released from something but I'm afraid even to breathe deeply. I just see the fields, the grey-brown hills and the trees in the woods and I can't imagine that there are other areas, landscapes or cities where I will go again. I want nothing more to do with it. So it is possible to live alone after all? It is possible to retreat from conventional life? They lied to me: I could have lived with Sibylle after all. It's true, the world wouldn't have agreed with me and I would have been punished. There are rules, said Erik. I hated him because he was stronger then I was. And yet I was convinced I felt genuine affection for him. Oh, I was convinced I'd never be jealous or even give room to such feelings. But it was he whom Sibylle had held in her arms, he whom Sibylle had released, and unscathed, he had carried on his way. He was unscathed, no one could accuse him of anything, he still loved Sibylle and she couldn't harm him. He told me that you had to realize some essential things in life: it had nothing to do with social prejudices, but in the first place with our soul, with our dependence on God. I was prepared to accept this and felt very guilty. But I am only human and it was all very well for him to say. He said the greatest sin was to divert one's energy away from God and to toss it into a void. No act of will or sacrifice was justified if not done for the greater good and towards fulfilment of one's true form.

'How do I know my true form?' I said.

'You have to believe that God loves you,' said Erik. 'Then you won't do anything that's beneath you.'

He was a devout person.

In the evening, I went to the English envoy's reception. It was crowded and I knew a good many of the people there. Everyone was very friendly, they asked after my work and said I should take a holiday to convalesce. An old gentleman whom I only knew in passing invited me to come and stay on his estate in East Prussia. I felt very well all evening and stayed quite late. There was a good buffet and plenty of champagne, and I sat talking to a couple of young Englishmen from the embassy. They spoke very good German and told me that young people in England were still poorly educated but that many were changing and were interested in other countries. They suggested I come with them to Oxford in summer to attend an English course. I thought it was a wonderful idea. One of the Englishmen wanted to leave soon after that and we left together. As I approached my car, Willy was standing there waiting for me. It suddenly struck me how wan and thin he looked, and that he needed looking after. 'Are you not freezing?' I asked. He said, 'I've been waiting here for an hour.' The young Englishman said goodbye. I think he was under the wrong impression about Willy and me.

We drove off. It was one o'clock. There was quite a lot of traffic. We drove past the Tiergarten, over the bridge and along Lützowufer.

'Sibylle isn't at the theatre,' Willy said suddenly. 'She's waiting for you in the bar.'

'Didn't she sing tonight?' I asked.

'She cancelled.'

'Did something happen?'

Willy looked straight ahead and murmured,

'She doesn't want me to tell you.'

'Nonsense,' I said. 'I'm her friend.'

'Yes, of course,' said Willy, comfortingly. 'But that's how she is. And now they're threatening to take the child away.'

He looked at me. I said nothing.

I experienced a very curious sensation. It was as if the earth had suddenly lost its gravitational pull and I'd been released. I clung to the steering wheel but my feet were far away, unmoored, and I was very light and empty and could have floated up through space. My breathing was so light that it was almost superfluous. Next to me, Willy said: 'The child is not her own but was taken in by Sibylle after the mother died.'

I had lived beside Sibylle, had seen her every day and had been preoccupied with her, and yet at the same time, she had been preoccupied by something quite different.

And now I'd found out and I felt empty when I should have felt almost relieved or comforted.

'Who is the child?' I asked. So I was right all along. She wasn't unfaithful to me. She hadn't been making fun of me.

She had a child.

'She did it for the father,' said Willy. 'No one knows about this. He was arrested for drug trafficking. She promised him she would look after the child. But she doesn't have any money.'

I drove slowly. The streets were slippery and dark. As I drove over crossroads, my headlamps were reflected off a side street and refracted across my windscreen.

'There are ways of getting money,' I said.

'But the driver is going to take the child away from her,' said Willy. 'He's the mother's brother. The court made him the guardian. He's allowed to.'

'Why doesn't she want to give up the child?' I asked.

'She says she doesn't want to live without the child,' said Willy gloomily.

'That's the way women are. She loves it.'

We parked the car a few houses away from the dive bar and covered the radiator.

'Go on ahead,' I said.

'No,' said Willy. 'She doesn't know that I fetched you.'

Then I asked abruptly:

'Why didn't you go to Erik?'

'He won't do anything,' said Willy.

'Sibylle doesn't want me to ask him for anything. She says he's her friend but he doesn't need to know everything.'

I felt slightly happier and a little less despondent. I walked quickly past the doorman. Sibylle was sitting at one of the front tables and smoking. She looked strikingly beautiful. She asked if I had eaten and ordered me a beer. Willy had stayed outside at the bar.

'What's the matter?' I asked. Sibylle looked searchingly at me and said 'Nothing. Nothing at all is the matter.'

We were like strangers. I felt it and was agitated, and I didn't know what to do. We sat for quite a while in silence.

'What about the child?' I ventured carefully.

'She's ill,' said Sibylle. 'I have to take her in again.'

'Will he give her to you?'

'You have to do something for me,' she said. 'I only thought of it today. You have to sign that you will provide for the child.'

I felt something in me go cold. My hands were cold too.

'I'd have to adopt her,' I said.

Sibylle said nothing.

'When do you have to know by?'

'Don't talk to anyone about this,' she said curtly. 'Ring me tomorrow.'

We went out, got into the car and drove off. I wanted to suggest that she come up to my apartment, I longed to have her to myself, to comfort her and bridge the gulf between us. But I was afraid of asking her at that particular moment because it would certainly have hurt her.

As we drove, she laid her hand on my neck and clasped it with her fingers. She didn't say a word.

'Is it very bad?' I asked.

'Yes,' she said. 'It's my life. But I knew they wouldn't let me keep her.'

'I'll help you,' I said. My voice was shaking. She clasped my neck more tightly.

'Darling,' she said. 'I know you won't help me. You're all the same, you can never help.'

By then, we were in front of her apartment. She got out, took the key from her bag, gave me her hand and went up the steps to the front door. There were three steps, and I just saw her slender legs and evening shoes through the low window of the car. She was wearing a short dress on that evening because she hadn't been on the stage.

I stayed at the wheel. I was somehow paralyzed.

When Sibylle saw that I hadn't pulled away, she came back and I opened the door for her. She sat next to me and pulled my head towards her.

'Perhaps I could grow to love you,' she said. 'But don't despair. I was very good for you. You'll realize that later.'

Who was being comforted here?

'I'm leaving,' she said. 'But perhaps you'd like to come with me?'

'Would it make you happy?' I asked in a strangled voice.

'Yes,' she said. 'I wouldn't suggest it otherwise.'

'We could take the child with us,' I said.

And then, my God, she smiled. She let go of my head and smiled. And Willy said she'd wept.

In the first place is our relationship to God.

Everything personal is meaningless.

You have to live according to your form.

Everything that distracts you from that is a sin.

There's no greater sin than being distracted from God.

And she'd wept!

By all means, there is no greater sin than letting Sibylle suffer.

'I'll do everything I can to help you,' I said. She said nothing more. She got out for a second time. And then I immediately drove away.

The next day, I spoke to a lawyer whom I knew through Erik. He said he would take on the matter and after I'd left, he rang up Magnus. He didn't deal with it in the correct manner but I'm sure he meant well. He also went to see Sibylle but she turned him away. When I wanted to speak to her that afternoon, her landlady said she was still asleep but I could go and meet her in the evening in the Walltheater. It was very hard to do anything for her. I felt very unwell all day and was sick several times. Erik sent me a doctor. He examined me and said my constitution was weakened and my gastric nerves were not working properly.

I tried once more to reach Sibylle. She came to the telephone and told me I shouldn't have done anything without asking her. 'Perhaps you're about to send the police over here,' she said. I'd forgotten that she never wanted to have anything to do with the police or any kind of official.

Then Erik rang me up. He wanted to tell my father. I screamed at him and begged him not to. I said: 'You've all gone mad!' But he probably thought *I'd* gone mad. I felt hatred towards Erik. At four o'clock, I called the maid and had an overnight bag packed.

I was in a state of dire confusion and believed that everything I wanted was wrong. I thought it would be better to go to my father and ask him to let me go away with Sibylle. But then I realized I would make myself look ridiculous. I would be treated like a school child. Then I resolved to talk to Sibylle. But she'd trusted me and I'd disappointed her, and that was all simple and clear.

I threw myself on the bed and was beside myself, not knowing a way out.

Then I put my coat on, took the overnight bag and went down to fetch the car.

I'd have liked to see Irmgard again. But I was afraid of relenting and I had to leave. I drove down a different street so as not to go past her house. It was already dark and it took nearly an hour to get out of the city.

Twenty-one

Yesterday, the hunters left. Now the dining room is closed and I eat in the parlour where locals play cards in the evenings. I write there and have a view onto the square. I think I'll be gone soon, perhaps even tomorrow. I'm going to tell the garage tonight. I wanted to read through what I've written so far. But then perhaps I won't like it. It was Sibylle I wrote it for, and she'll probably never read it.

I've had coffee. It's three o'clock. I'd still like to go for a walk and so I cross over to the park.

At seven o'clock in the evening, the main gate is closed but on the other side of the lake, there isn't a gate, the woods start and if you go further, you come to the public road that goes right through the middle of the woods, connecting the isolated villages.

I keep near to the palace tonight. It's very calm among the trees and the ground is soft and covered in needles like a carpet. Inside the park, the paths sometimes come to an end, the thicket becomes dense and you have to fight your way through laboriously. I'd like to come out at the end of the park but this takes some time, and now and again I think I've lost my way and that I'm heading back towards the palace or the water's edge.

But all of a sudden, I arrive and step out into the open. It comes as something of a surprise. I can see the overcast sky low over the brown fields that stretch to the horizon. In the woods, it was warm and the air was light and breezy; here, the wind gusts powerfully around me, everything is potent and the flatland begins right at my feet and extends outwards like a huge river. Above me, the trees are being thrashed by the wind and the rushing noise is like the wing beats of a great flock of birds ascending into the sky. I lean my back against a trunk. Here the woods begin and end, here is earth and the smell of earth, and leaves beneath my feet. And here is the wind and an infinite stretch of land, a blend of muted tones, and there will be cold and then warmth again, and the earth will crack, fruits will force it open and ripen.

And I feel like going away from this place.

I think about the sea. It's not far. In just a few hours, I could be on the Baltic Coast. I would look at the ships in the harbour, and the sailors, and I could drink with the sailors and sail out with them. Or I could return to the city. I could be friends with Magnus again and study in the library. And everything would be like it was before. I've made up my mind and I don't need to feel ashamed of myself in front of others. They said I was never able to make up my mind: now I have, and I'm content. Now I know what life's like: you don't get anything without making a sacrifice. That's justice.

I take out my wallet and count the notes inside. I have a little over three hundred marks. I can go far on that. Everything is fine.

I think of the city, of Magnus, of Irmgard and my work—I imagine it all in detail, the streets, the path through the Tiergarten, the early evening fog, my apartment and the lit-up reading room in the library. I think too about whether I'll go back to the Walltheater.

And then, all of a sudden, it hits me with force: Sibylle won't be there any more. I'm still leaning against the tree, and now I need to grip it. How could I forget this? I'd gone away, knowing what that meant. But it hadn't been clear to me.

And so nothing matters. I want to lie down on the ground and not think any more. It's all the same if everything comes to an end for Sibylle isn't there any more. It's all the same if people like me or if I'm successful. What's the use, for they took Sibylle away from me, and nothing will ever replace her. So this is sacrifice and justice. But I don't understand the first thing about it; I am just blind with pain. Didn't she have a child whom she loved more than me? But she wanted me to help her and then she could have kept the child. And she'd have known how much I love her. Now it's too late. So much life before me and it's too late for this one thing. I will live without Sibylle, but it hadn't been clear to me.

I won't drive to the sea.

I won't drink with sailors.

I won't give Sibylle these pages.

When I return, she won't be there.

AFTERWORD

'THE SINCERITY, DIGNITY AND HAPPINESS OF EXISTENCE'

Everybody's youth is a dream,
a form of chemical madness.

F. Scott Fitzgerald, *The Diamond as Big as the Ritz*

The novella, its 'main flaw' and the critics

Klaus Mann was right. The 'mood of the times' was simply 'not favourable' for *Lyric Novella* which was published in Berlin in the spring of 1933. Hitler had recently seized power in Germany, and subsequent events spoilt any chances of the book being widely read, let alone acclaimed.

Few critics gave a favourable verdict. Some praised the beauty of its language and the talent of the author but also criticized its 'pervasuce atmosphere of social insouciance' (Klaus Mann). Apart from Mann, perhaps only Carl Seelig perceived the artistic ability and emotional conflicts which lay behind this apparently harmless and traditional love story ('Which young Swiss talent dares these days to write as personally as Annemarie Schwarzenbach?'). Others, such as Eduard Korrodi, the influential critic from *Neue Züricher Zeitung* (who had praised *Freunde um Bernhard*, Schwarzenbach's first book), rejected it as worthless ('We see no need for such lightweight narrative efforts'). Literature professor Charles Clarac, who too was otherwise well disposed towards Schwarzenbach, urged her to write 'quelque chose plus humaine' ('something more humane'). Perplexed by these critiques, Schwarzenbach wrote to Clarac on 15 June 1933: 'The need for serious decisions has now become so urgent, difficult and radical for each and every one of us that the sentimental crises of twenty-year-olds are bound to appear trivial.' She believed that 'we *will* write on more difficult topics now, the times are too difficult for one to dare or even have fun writing something frivolous.' Nevertheless, she wanted to portray 'outsiders' in her next book even more strongly, 'with more objectivity, less personally, but also more powerfully and confidently'. According to her, the 'main flaw' of the novella was that 'the twenty-year-old hero is not a hero, not a young man, but a young girl—that should have been made clear so as to avoid the dangers of confusion, and to make this difficult insight more human, truthful and plausible.'

Seen from this angle, the novella today holds a particular fascination as an early portrayal of lesbian love. The homosexual nature of the relationship is not mentioned openly in the book but will be obvious to sensitive readers as it is thinly veiled. It is not clear, however, whether the true nature of the relationship was noticed by the critics (who were, incidentally, all male) nor whether it played a part in their moral indignation. What is clear is that Schwarzenbach's practice of disguising lesbian love as a heterosexual relationship is one that can be detected even in her earlier writing. Reasons for this may be found in the author's biography on the one hand and in literary tradition on the other.

Schwarzenbach had virtually no female role models at the time to portray her subject matter. Like Marcel Proust or Klaus Mann, she hid her homosexuality in her writing by forcing herself into a corset of gender norms, perhaps hoping to thus reach a wider audience. An openly lesbian love story would certainly not have been published by Rowohlt Verlag at the time.

The issues in *Lyric Novella* are closely linked to Schwarzenbach's personal situation in Berlin, and to the city's social and literary environment. The key to understanding the background of that era in Berlin, however, lies in Schwarzenbach's beginnings as a writer (1925–31), in the complex relationship she had with her mother, in the strong influence of the priest, Ernst Merz, and later of Erika and Klaus Mann, as well as in her early writings and letters.

The influence of Ernst Merz

'It was on a beautiful autumn day in the year 1924 that she attended a youth rally in Rein bei Brugg. I gave a lecture, entitled "Loneliness, Friendship and Community", to an open-minded group of people. My words must have enthused the sixteen-year-old because she promptly expressed her wish to be taught and confirmed by me.' This is how priest and writer, Ernst Merz (1886–1977), describes his first meeting with the young Schwarzenbach, a seminal experience for both. Years later, Merz could remember the personality trait that went on to mark her whole life, and which was, by the time of their meeting, already evident: 'My pupil set about discussing vital questions with an unparalleled liveliness and open-mindedness, and attempted

—although our roles were somewhat reversed, to account for everything, down to the very last detail.' The themes of Merz' lecture that Schwarzenbach listened to as a member of the Wandervogel[1] would influence her for the rest of her life. She tried, for example, to repeatedly rekindle the 'fire of youth's power' as invoked by Merz even when her youth was long gone. Merz, who had connections to the circle around the poet Stefan George (1868–1933) and avidly admired him, also acquainted Schwarzenbach with his works.

Merz himself was deeply influenced by his teacher, Leonhard Ragaz. This controversial theologist associated a 'radical commitment to the problems of the proletariat with a staunch pacifism and a kind of doctrine of salvation on the imminent advent of the Kingdom of God' (Thomas Karlauf). Without doubt, Merz passed some of Ragaz' views on to Schwarzenbach and they too seemed to have had a profound effect on her. Her political and religious views in the 1930s can be partially understood as an echo of those of Ragaz, and it is astounding how similar both their views were in criticizing Switzerland's stance during the Second World War.

It is equally astounding that the Schwarzenbach clan, many of whose members were in the military, agreed to send the young Schwarzenbach to a pacifist for confirmation lessons. At that time, Schwarzenbach's mother still displayed a certain tolerance towards her beloved daughter. For she was not unaware of the attitude of the priest ('Anti-militarism won't wash with me, as you know'). Perhaps she under-estimated the capacity of her precocious child to absorb new things; perhaps she regarded the Bible as no more than a missive, detached from the real world and without any power to affect or intervene in current sociopolitical issues. In reality, it was Merz' 'teachings' that sowed the seeds of Schwarzenbach's later conflicts with her family.

Merz, himself a homosexual, was so taken with his pupil, twelve years his junior, that his 1928 diary records the contemplation of a life shared with her. He also intended to dedicate a chapter to her in a book he was thinking of writing about his friends, both alive and dead. Though its publication was planned for 1930, it was never written (his memoirs of Schwarzenbach were first printed in 1985). In his *Das Reich neuer Jugend* (The Realm of New Youth), published in 1928, in which 'a new community is called up, whose spirit should be the spirit of George' (Thomas Karlauf), Merz must have talked too much about 'leadership' and 'dependency' for Schwarzenbach who hankered after freedom. Merz, who worked in the Rein parish in the canton of Aargau, remained true to his values and refused to give a field chaplain the pulpit for a sermon and thus caused a great public stir. This and other reasons led him to resign from the priesthood in the same year. At the end of the 1930s, he moved to Tessin where he worked as a writer and community mayor. Contact with his earnest pupil seems to have broken off around this time.

The Wandervogel and the status of girls

For Schwarzenbach, the period of the Wandervogel (1924–25) represented the first step away from the influence of her parents and towards some kind of independence. It was also then that she 'discovered' nature; later, nature (as a place of self-realization) would become one of the overriding motifs of her oeuvre. And it was in the *Wandervogel* newspaper that she published her first articles.

What attracted Schwarzenbach to the Wandervogel? Merz, who was close to the movement but not part of it, once defined it as 'an outsized love and worship of nature', a backdrop for romantic longing. According to him, the movement was not only romantic but also a 'justified outrage against everything mechanized, unanimated or with a false form or quality'. And, most importantly, 'the association has no strong political views; however, it takes for granted the rejection of war and a certain "socialism".' This certain 'socialism' was keenly experienced by Schwarzenbach: she was, for the first time, part of a community that was not driven by the privileged status of its individual members. She was certainly impressed by the way 'youth' as a 'lifestyle' was taken seriously, and this could quite easily have led to a criticism of 'the sacred family life at school and in church' (Merz) and of the various rites that she rediscovered in the works of George.

'Zur Mädchenfrage' (On the Question of Girls, 1925) is one of her most interesting texts written around this time and dealing with a theme that was characteristic of her: the situation of girls in the midst of the superiority of boys. The essay provocatively calls to the Wandervogel girls to leave the association because 'two major things are missing: leadership and friendship.' In order to be a 'personality', girls needed more than the celebration of traditions such as 'romanticism, journeys and song evenings': they had to 'set their sights beyond the Wandervogel'. Otherwise, their existence, 'half liberated, but still dependent on boys', would lack its most important aspect and be 'devoid of ideas and works, without love and beauty'. For Schwarzenbach, beauty was linked to autonomy and independence; when she freely associated it with aesthetics, she seemed to be developing her own female point of view and form. That women should be 'a force', and indeed were, when their identities were not shaped exclusively by men, was already undisputed for the seventeen-year-old Schwarzenbach.

Her struggle to find an identity, however, rubbed itself raw on both male and female realities. In letters to Merz, her confidante, she complained that, above all, *male* attributes were missing in women: 'Women are not capable of profundity. They are petty and gossipy [. . .] Not one of them is truly passionate, truly a victim, or truly familiar to me. Most of them live for a man [. . .] And their greatest strengths only develop through him' (1929). In her accusation about women's inadequacy with regard to 'intellectual work', however, she underestimates her own intellectual power in making this judgement. Equally, she overestimates male intellect and the world of men, which is not surprising in view of the extremely hierarchical milieu of her home. She felt, in equal measure, both constrained and stimulated by the male spirit of her family environment; and she veered in her work between the extremes of a lost identity and sovereignty. Schwarzenbach was brought up under the fierce protection of her mother, whose Prussian culture meant that she trained her daughter to assume a masculine reserve; this made it doubly difficult for Schwarzenbach to discover her true self.

Her search for an identity is evident in her early writing —*Pariser Novelle I und II* (1929) and *Paris III* (1930). It is in *Pariser Novelle II,* one of her most autobiographical works, that she most especially rebels against a feminine identity shaped by masculine notions. The female narrator in the novel is attracted to a man who has travelled widely and who writes, drawn by an 'intellectual passion'. When she is lonely, she writes him a sort of love letter in which she categorically denies any possibility for loving a man: 'Incidentally, you are so sure of yourself, so conceited in your hyper-criticism, so endlessly alone due to your knowledge. [...] For I also believe that you are a bad person. Weak, vain and wicked, like all men, because they do not have the same humility as we women do.' When she meets him again, she rejects any kind of claim he has on her. To a woman whom she loves she confesses that he has taken away her 'freedom to love', since 'without him, I was nothing. My emotions were nothing, except if they were his; my faith was nothing, except if confirmed by his judgement.' But her love for this woman founders on convention and family morality. When both women visit relatives in Switzerland, the host forbids their sleeping in the same room. The narrator leaves, alone, a single sentence repeating itself in her mind: 'With beautiful women came justice and injustice.'

The Rosenkavalier and the 'suffering cavalier'

Beautiful women—principally from the upper bourgeoisie and aristocracy—would visit the Schwarzenbach home in Bocken when Annemarie was a child. The proud mother would present her favourite daughter to the ladies during tea parties and the child would be cosseted and spoilt. When one beautiful lady displayed her affection too strongly, the young girl blushed at the gesture and looked to her mother for help. Her mother, however, sent her out of the room, a decision Annemarie felt was unfair. This feeling of being punished for something that her mother had essentially arranged confused her to the end of her life and robbed her of trust.

Apparently, Renée Schwarzenbach had nearly bled to death during Annemarie's birth. Perhaps that is why she almost suffocated the child with love, 'seeing her own image in her from the outset' (Suzanne Oehman). She had always wanted to be a boy; now, she brought her daughter up as one. She even encouraged Annemarie's infatuations with women provided, of course, they remained infatuations. She herself had an infatuation for Emmy Krüger, the Wagner singer, whose career in Zurich had begun with the role of the Rosenkavalier and who always stayed at the Schwarzenbach home when she was in Switzerland.

Which child does not like to dress up? And so, with Krüger in mind, Renée dressed her daughter as the Rosenkavalier who, at the end of the opera, is revealed to be a man dressed as a woman. Renée also turned everyday life into a theatrical spectacle: Annemarie had to bow before Krüger and offer her a rose. The scene was repeated every evening as in the theatre: two Rosenkavaliers, and, between them, the 'born mistress' (Gerhard Spinner). But Renée placed Annemarie in other roles too, though always male ones: soldier, page and sailor. Later, Annemarie was left with one role that cannot be played—that of self-destruction.

How does one escape the almost violent love of a mother whose name in 1929 still sounded to Schwarzenbach 'like music' (*Pariser Novelle I*)? How does one escape the strength and charisma of a woman who is not only a mother but also the leader of a powerful clan? As a young girl, Schwarzenbach dreamt of becoming a general when she grew up, no doubt inspired by her grandfather. Like her idolized mother, however, she too had the burning desire to do as she wished and thereby solve all life's problems, as if in a dream. The twenty-one-year-old Schwarzenbach expresses this through her female narrator in *Pariser Novelle II* who says that she 'does not have *the right* to choose freely. "I am nothing." There is only my duty and what he calls "home".' And 'home' means the mother. She, the clan, is *everything* and the world. In the same text, the narrator asks: 'Must one's world be destroyed in order to build a new one?' Yes, it must, Schwarzenbach would answer, but at the cost of extreme loneliness and self-sacrifice. Tormented by this moral dilemma, her only escape lay in suffering, in drug-induced intoxication and in writing. Hurt, abandoned mothers can only be appeased if pain is offered up to them in art 'like a sacrifice' (*Pariser Novelle I*). However, 'guilt lies much deeper': all the suffering in the world will not retrieve what has been lost. All her life, she offered up her pain—in the role of the 'suffering cavalier'—like roses to her mother.

Did Schwarzenbach really have no chance of forging her own path? In *Freunde um Bernhard*, she depicts her efforts and difficulties through the character of Bernhard who, 'despite his gentle nature, [. . .] was stubborn and defiant in his demands. Worse than this, was his [. . .] tendency to choose his own friends.' Afraid of the bad influence

of his friends Gert and Ines, Bernhard's parents send him
to Paris. Similarly, in 1925, Schwarzenbach was sent to
school in remote Ftan, not because she wished to go but
because of an 'incident'. This 'incident'—which caused a stir
in the whole family—seems to have been an intense infatuation for another girl. Schwarzenbach was thereafter
closely watched by her family every time she tried to make
friends outside the domestic circle. More and more, she was
regarded as an 'outsider who was attached by some invisible
threads to other worlds and was therefore both endangered
and a danger, in some way that was not yet evident' (*Freunde
um Bernhard*). These vulnerable yet wild aspects of her
nature intensified when she met Erika and Klaus Mann.

'In their heart of hearts, they do not agree with me'

It was with Erika Mann that Schwarzenbach was at last
able to take up the fight against her family and its constrain-
ing traditions. They met in 1930. It is not clear how exactly
the relationship began but Schwarzenbach immediately
loved and idolized the self-confident Erika and showered
her with all the devotion that had formerly been coveted by
her overbearing mother. In fact, at the beginning of their
relationship, Erika was assigned the role of a second mother:
Schwarzenbach would end her letters to Erika with 'Your
child' ('Dein Kind') although Erika was only three years
older. Perhaps she meant 'very youthful' or 'inexperienced'
and perhaps this is also why Klaus Mann called her
'Schweizerkind' ('Swiss child'). It was not long before
Schwarzenbach drifted into the same fatal dependency on
Erika: her idolization of the 'goddess of liberation' put her at

Erika's beck and call, and Erika occasionally exploited this. How intense Erika's feelings truly were towards her friend could only have been testified by the letters she wrote, but these were later destroyed by Renée.

Erika was a crucial source of support for Schwarzenbach as she struggled to become an artist and political activist despite her family's every attempt to the contrary. With her brother Klaus, Erika introduced Schwarzenbach to a circle of artists whose driving influences were homosexuality and drugs. Schwarzenbach's family considered this other 'leftist' world a strong threat and Renée saw in Erika a rival whose influence on Annemarie was stronger than her own. Erika was made to pay for this: in Zurich, 1934, it was Renée who allegedly organized the pro-fascist, Swiss Frontist attacks on Pfeffermühle, Erika's cabaret theatre. It was only then that the mother–daughter symbiosis was violently shaken, if not broken.

When it was certain that Schwarzenbach wanted to put herself in Erika and Klaus' care and move to Berlin in 1931, the family household in Bocken exploded into scenes reminiscent of a Strindberg play or a Greek tragedy. (Later, at Renée's funeral, the priest Gerhard Spinner described her as someone 'from another century' who tried to turn the entire family against the renegade Annemarie by plotting and scheming, and who saw a new threat in almost every one of Annemarie's acquaintances.) 'The entire house is overwrought, hopeless and dismal,' wrote Schwarzenbach to Erika in 1931, and she was stricken with new feelings of guilt as she observed her mother becoming entrenched in 'suspicious, bitter isolation' ('Mama must be one of the unhappiest people alive'). Schwarzenbach grew even less convinced that she would ever find happiness.

In his *Der Vulkan* (1938), Klaus Mann immortalized the memory of this love–hate mother–daughter relationship: Renée and Annemarie were transformed into an Amsterdam hotelkeeper and her daughter, Stinchen. The novel contained 'inordinately violent scenes' between Stinchen and the 'unmaternal mother, as broad and wide-legged as a grenadier' who 'grumbled, raged, chastised, scolded and wept'. Also, 'the jealousy with which this mannish old woman dogged Stinchen seemed suspiciously extreme. [. . .] This was no longer the natural concern of a mother for her daughter's virtue: rather, it was the tense, passionate, wild wakefulness of lovers.'

Alfred, Schwarzenbach's father, seems to have disappeared behind the dominant presence of Renée's intimate friend Krüger, and was apparently often away 'on business'. In some (verified) cases, he showed a somewhat less conservative attitude than his wife and preferred to side with his daughter. He does not, however, figure prominently in Schwarzenbach's writing and letters. In a letter written in 1930, Schwarzenbach penned these prophetic sentences regarding her conflict with her family: 'In their heart of hearts, they do not agree with me and never will. Even the brothers.' As if to underscore its significance, this sentence appears almost verbatim in her *Freunde um Bernhard.* As early as 1929, Schwarzenbach clearly recognized the array of problems she faced, as shown by an assertion (made by the friend of her alter ego, Ursula) in *Pariser Novelle II*: 'Your mother will never understand that you are a free spirit. You can't work in an environment stifled by tradition. Forcing yourself to show respect would exhaust you, rob you of your best. Your mother will never understand that.'

But alongside this insight lay something else: loyalty, both to her family and to tradition.

'Lied der Wunde' (Song of the Wound) Sonja Sekula

'We are looking for a new heaven and earth,' wrote the seventeen-year-old Schwarzenbach with reference to a text by Merz in his guest book. Like no other sentence, this sums up the limitlessness (and inevitable failure) of Schwarzenbach's search for the 'source of purity', a search she explains thus: 'It is truly an illness in me: I want to know everything' (*Pariser Novelle I*). But she wanted the world to understand that this statement referred to a desire for 'meaning'—not mere curiosity. In her search for innocence, and with 'God's forgiveness' in mind, she was willing to make almost any sacrifice in exchange for the adventure of self-discovery and the acquisition of worldly wisdom. She was even prepared to forgo happiness, which she equated with 'stagnancy or slackness' ('Stellung der Jugend', 1930). 'When I'm happy, I'm as small as all the rest and I can't bear that. That's why I want greatness, painful greatness,' she wrote in a letter in 1926. Again and again, she would seek 'a meaning, a God, truth' in 'all the suffering of the world' (*Pariser Novelle II*). But where does the greatness of suffering lead? Her pain and the pity of her friends for their 'suffering cavalier' were great. But how could she escape this role? Once she was seized by the 'virtue of intellectual passion' that she described as an 'obsession', she was pulled almost magnetically towards 'distress'. This is 'firstly, profundity. Bring forth your profundity' ('Gespräch', 1928). And so she developed— as a means of insight—a tangible logic of failure, an art of destruction for herself.

Schwarzenbach's yearning 'to do nothing but travel, from world to world' (1926), coupled with an apparently self-destructive impulse for knowledge and the drive towards 'suffering greatness' had manifested themselves even *before* her conflict with the family. However, she seems to have made suffering the principle by which she lived and experienced the world, perhaps because she was helpless in the face of her over-dominant mother and her own political convictions. Are insanity and suicide the only escape routes for sensitive, rebellious daughters suffocated by the love of their mothers? Perhaps this is why female artists such as Sylvia Plath, Unica Zürn or the Swiss painter-writer, Sonja Sekula (1918–63) with whom Schwarzenbach had much in common, developed an 'aesthetic pain'. Sekula, for example, wrote: 'I am the green, dark sister—I am the shrill call of the afflicted, I am fear, I am noise and pain [. . .] I am the boat moored, the long wait, the self-visitation' (*Lied der Wunde*).

Consolation and the terrain of writing

'We want neither desire, nor apathy: we want works of art' ('Stellung der Jugend'): Schwarzenbach tried, with this almost callous rigorousness, to locate and fulfil the 'meaning' she longed for in art, especially in literature. It was in a work of art more than anything, in a successful 'harmony of colours, words and nuances' ('Stellung der Jugend'), that she could perceive a part of 'God's perfection.' Art offers the only place for the endless motion of life to meet the artist's restlessness and longing. Klaus had similar ideas: in his 1927 essay 'Heute und Morgen', he explained his ambition for his books to take up the 'dynamism of life' and be 'filled to overflowing with life's beauty, life's grief, and its sublime, restless, wonderful banality'.

Schwarzenbach found in writing the ultimate medium to help discover her identity and the world and with which to maintain an 'illusion of permanence', at least on the surface. Forced into masculine roles by her mother and providing a multi-projection medium for others, she was, in her writing, finally able to pull the strings and allocate roles according to her fancy (this can be observed, above all, in *Freunde um Bernhard*). Writing was the perfect place for her to make manifest the constant tension 'between loneliness and community' without which nothing is 'lively, beneficial and rich in pain' ('Gespräch'). As a writer, she was intimate with her characters and yet distant from them—an experience that reflected her primary experience in love. And doesn't the writer feel at once close and distant to herself as well?

Evidently, the prospect of writing was Schwarzenbach's only assurance of 'the sincerity, dignity and happiness of existence' (1931). And she felt consoled after she wrote a 'good page' although the hardships of life had not been minimized. She felt the happiness of being able to comfort herself with words for she often missed Erika's or her mother's affection. Language was a constantly accessible medium, a drug that she was addicted to (and not only to its consoling properties) but that did not make her ill. This intoxication seems to be linked to her notion that language was rather like a musical movement. As early as 1925, she had observed to Merz that 'the mere type, sound and beauty of a word' gave her joy:

> I almost never write for the sake of an idea, but rather, a thought emerges at some point, giving me merely the foundation and the medium to be able to write. The subject matter comes of its own accord, but to write, to form, slowly, making music, as it were, that gives me a feeling of happiness.

'Land cannot be taken away,' wrote Schwarzenbach in *Lyric Novella*. The topography that she created in her writing could not be seized from her either. It is no wonder that Renée was suspicious of her daughter's writing: a printed text escaped her influence. The written word was irrefutable and, for Renée, this must have been a demonstration of her powerlessness. She had her revenge here too and burnt part of her daughter's work after her death. Schwarzenbach's letters and diaries were *the* secret chamber into which her mother's gaze never penetrated. By destroying them, Renée destroyed Annemarie's circle of friends and their 'world' and, unwittingly, also a large part of her daughter.

Klaus Mann and the 'Stellung der Jugend'

In December 1930, an evening of lectures and readings was organized by the Zurich Student Council in conjunction with the Manns and Schwarzenbach at the Eidgenössische Technische Hochschule (Swiss Federal Institute of Technology) on the theme of 'New German Writing'. It was there that Schwarzenbach met the Manns for the first time.

Schwarzenbach had, in 1929, written a very positive review of their book *Abenteuer*. If she admired in Erika qualities such as courage and independence, which she felt were missing in Klaus, she found in him a soulmate who had similar notions about life and art. He had suffered in the shadow of his successful father as she had had to struggle with her dominant mother. Both were vulnerable personalities because of their almost over-developed sensitivity. Their friendship lasted right up to Annemarie's death, despite occasional differences over politics and Annemarie's great internal conflicts. Their fates strangely coincided—between Annemarie's bicycle accident in September 1942 and her death in November 1942—despite their not having seen one another for almost two years. Klaus, as if he had heard about and internalized the tragic incident, wrote in his diary on 24 October 1942: 'Terrible sadness—overshadowing everything. Wish for death' (*Der Wendepunkt*). This wish was repeated several times over the next few days. And after Annemarie's death, he went on to enlist in the American army, as if he wanted to throw himself into a bleak military existence.

The world 'which allowed a world war to develop is bad', Schwarzenbach wrote in 'Stellung der Jugend', an essay in which she tried to sum up the attitude of a German-speaking 'lost generation' (Gertrude Stein). It was a 'period of transformation' in which 'all forms of order' had dissolved and youth, 'full of all the weaknesses of the post-war period', could only be criticized: 'We [. . .] are outsiders and vagabonds, utterly insecure, utterly without foundation, knowing no bounds nor greatness.' This characterization of youth, lacking in any positive values, appears to be a reaction to the increasingly hollow notions of 'morality, custom and society' from a generation of parents who were separated from the young because of their 'difference in "world view".'

Was Annemarie familiar with Klaus' essay 'Heute und Morgen' that pre-empts many of the reflections in hers? Both wrote about the great schism in the young generation, a generation united only in its helplessness and search for a goal; the new world view is, above all, one of 'grace', Klaus' key term for his and Annemarie's world experience:

> To be pious in life means to have grace. To have grace means, above all, to be in love with all things—with the wide landscape, with the slenderness of the human body. To revere a human body with all the boundless melancholy, all the unconscious devotion with which one reveres the secret of an eventful life. Not wanting to possess the revered body, but constantly thank it for being there and breathing. Not wanting to possess that life, remain strange in it—but, beyond melancholy, constantly to thank God that one is alive ('Heute und Morgen').

Klaus perceived 'grace' in Stefan George's works, particularly in his *Liebeslyrik* (Love Poems). Klaus and Annemarie must have come across George's work by the time Klaus was attending the Odenwaldschule (1922–23) and Annemarie was in the Wandervogel. George was the guiding star for both in the first years of their writing, alongside Hölderlin, Nietzsche and Rilke, drawn as they were to his 'human-artistic dignity' (Klaus Mann), his appreciation of art as the aestheticization of life and his cult of friendship and youth. Both Klaus and Annemarie tried to maintain youth's open-

ness and apprehension when faced with the challeng
ageing (an experience made easier thanks to the pros
of their social class). 'Youth' was a form of self-de
Growing older and becoming an adult meant shoulc
the same responsibility and the same guilt as their p
In addition, Mann and Schwarzenbach were forced t
sonify 'eternal youth' and play the role of dependent ch
practical reasons: it was the only way to guarantee
financial support from their parents, right up to the
their lives. In this context, Walter Benjamin described the
circle around Klaus Mann as 'a microcosm of false child-
hoods, in which people detach themselves from existence'.

The ideological and material compulsion to remain
youthful, the distance they perceived between themselves
and other young people who felt drawn to a political party
or aesthetic direction, and the outsider role assumed due to
their homosexuality and drug addiction, led Klaus and
Annemarie to feel a kind of isolation that even an antifascist
commitment could not assuage. The glorification of this
loneliness could not always be avoided by either, not even
when Annemarie wrote: 'One should forbid young people
calling themselves lonely' (*Freunde um Bernhard*). Nevertheless, her faith in youth was not shaken in 1930 nor at any
time thereafter: 'Youth is always victorious', she wrote in
Paris III. It seems that Benjamin was mistaken when he
said of George that 'the old bourgeoisie disguises the pre-
sentiment of its weakness by rhapsodizing cosmically in all
spheres and, drunk on the future, misuses "youth" as an incan-
tatory word.'

'Youth and radicalism' (*Klaus Mann*)

Prior to 1933, Annemarie and Klaus occasionally manoeu-vred themselves into aestheticized isolation with their theories on society and art. But they were aware of their 'social duty' (Klaus Mann) even if their lifestyles often did nothing to confirm this. As 'a member of a highly endan-gered community', Klauss wrote in 1927 ('Heute und Morgen'), one is 'lost' if one forgets 'others' on one's 'lonely adventures'. The cosmopolitan-minded, prescient author recognized at an early stage how the extreme right- and left-wing political organizations, who exerted a great influence on his generation, were trying to do away with democracy and the individual in both Germany and abroad. Many of these organizations adorned themselves with a youthful aura and disguised their inhumane intentions with claims of heralding the future. It was because of this that, in 1930, Klaus objected to Stefan Zweig's all-too-eager 'willingness towards youth' (and thus went unwittingly against Anne-marie's statement on youth's victorious nature) and said: 'Not everything that youth does leads us into the future.' He was, of course, referring to the radicalism of the National Socialists.

Schwarzenbach first encountered her initially harmless Swiss comrades in 1930, during her studies at Zurich Uni-versity where, catalyzed by the global economic crisis and political revivalist movements abroad, the politicization of young academics had already begun. Right-wing students began to make a name for themselves through groups such as the Neue Front (which went on to merge with the fascist National Front in 1933), and the organ of the student body, the Zürcher Student, led from 1931 to 1933 by subsequent Frontist leader Robert Tobler, was mostly 'referred to as a political community' (Beat Glaus). Rolf Henne, later federal state leader of the National Front, wrote in a November 1932 essay about 'the young generation's great longing for community', a line which sounds like a quotation from either Annemarie or Klaus. (Incidentally, Henne was in love with Schwarzenbach and apparently sent her numerous, conspicuously coloured love letters, all of which she left unopened.)

Schwarzenbach's notion of 'community', however, had nothing to do with that of her admirer and his comrades. The New Front's 'Manifesto of Fraternity', published in June 1931 in Zürcher Front, stated: 'Equality and freedom nevertheless resist an organic development of community in which not all members can be leaders at the same time [. . .] We demand acknowledgement of the principle of elitism and space for responsible leaders in the community.' Schwarzenbach's 'In Praise of Freedom', published in April 1931 in the same newspaper, reads like a flaming riposte to its undemocratic demands: even in this 'hour of dictatorship', the 'confusion of political attitude and spiritual ways of life' was 'unbearable and humiliating'. Turning against the 'intolerant fanatics' and 'worshippers of authoritative faith', she asks: 'Should the efficiency of citizens be the prevailing standard for the "worth" of others?' And then supplies the answer herself: 'Humanity, tolerance and a pure will remain the natural demands of a free spirit, throughout all shifting forms of existence.'

After Hitler seized power, the word 'youth' assumed a terrible reality for Schwarzenbach in Germany. On 8 April 1933, she recalled in a letter to Klaus a connection between the yearning that they and the members of the youth movement had expressed for a 'community' and a 'leader', and the abuse of that yearning by the National Socialists:

> In the end, these uniformed street robbers and mercenaries, with their barbaric rowdiness, are, in fact, the same people who a few years ago set off to play ball and paper boats with their girlfriends at the weekends—and if they'd had no reason, they would have remained impervious to the temptations of mob orators—

'In big, dirt-spattered Berlin'

Schwarzenbach left Switzerland for Berlin on 19 September 1931. There are two photographs that capture her departure from Bocken and both show her standing in front of her 'Victory' car. In one, she is smiling (hardly ever the case in photographs), has her hands folded across her waist and looks like the innocent and loveable 'Schweizerkind' who would, later, carefully garage the car. The other is quite different: she looks more like a female Buster Keaton and wears her 'standard' serious (and later sad) expression, her gaze stubborn and challenging. Her right hand grips the door handle, her right foot rests lightly on the running board. As if she were about to climb in and strike another resolute pose for the photographer, her mother. Or is this determined posture simply a disguise for an undefined fear?

Nothing will hold Schwarzenbach back any longer, not even a window in her parent's house—visible behind the car—that remains enticingly open. She is, in her mind, already on the road, driving towards Berlin and the future. The bright lights and the misery of the big city—she was to experience both. And the two photographs, with their opposite moods, represent the two poles of her life in Berlin.

Schwarzenbach's 'official' reason for going to Berlin was to write an academic paper with the aid of her professor and mentor, Carl J. Buckhardt. Once in Berlin, she dedicated her time to two activities: the 'discipline' of writing, and love. Her wish to live as a writer could best be fulfilled away from her oppressive home in an anonymous, culturally vibrant city: 'in Berlin, there are libraries, publishers, journalists and it is, for the moment, neutral territory' (1931). It was surely an attraction for Schwarzenbach that Berlin, alongside Paris at the beginning of the 1930s, was still 'a centre of the lesbian world' (Ilse Kokula).

In April 1931, she had proved her academic excellence by finishing her studies in history with a doctorate thesis. She had evidently finished this work quickly, for it appeared almost simultaneously alongside *Freunde um Bernhard*. Then she spent her first joint holiday with Erika and Klaus in Bandol on the Côte d'Azur in May 1931. Her friendship with the Manns and the effortless holiday atmosphere must have made her decision to leave home that much easier. It was through the Manns that she got to know the illustrator Eva Herrmann, and the writer Wilhelm Speyer and his wife with whom she went on to become friends in Berlin.

Months before she left for Germany, she wrote about 'big, dirt-spattered Berlin'. This, and the fact that Berlin was one of the settings in *Freunde um Bernhard* (despite there being no actual descriptions of the city) suggest that she had already visited the capital.

How did Schwarzenbach experience everyday life in Berlin? Did she see the 'dirt' on the streets and in politics? Was she 'spattered' by it? Were her impressions similar to those of the committed French writer and philosopher Simone Weil, who wrote about her visit to Berlin in August–September 1932:

> Five and a half million people and their children live in poverty thanks to woefully insufficient help from the state and communities. More than two million are a burden on their families, beg or steal. Old men with mandarin collars and stiff hats, who have worked their whole lives as professionals, beg at underground station entrances or sing abject songs on the streets. But the tragedy lies less in this misery than in the circumstances that no person, even an energetic one, can have the slightest hope of escaping from this situation with his own strength ('Deutschland in Erwartung', Germany in Anticipation).

Did Schwarzenbach see the putsch coming, when, in July 1932, the Reich government deposed the Prussian government led by Social Democrat Otto Braun and revoked practically all basic rights? Writing to Erika during that Berlin period, Schwarzenbach mentioned political events only in passing. Like Klaus, she refused to 'admit that some party, a gang of opportunists and fanatics that boastfully call themselves "National Socialists"' should be capable of defying the entire stock of Western values and traditions' (*The Turning Point*). Rather, it was preferable to question oneself, 'against a backdrop of fireworks going off, from which we so harmlessly kept our distance' (1934). Despite the fraught circumstances, it was still possible in 1931–32 to lead a relatively normal life in Germany; if one was prosperous, it was even possible to enjoy it. Being Swiss, Schwarzenbach was not directly affected by the events in Germany. Later, however, she felt a commitment almost greater than that of her German emigrant friends with regard to the cultural heritage of their country. She was, nevertheless, not unaware of what was happening, even though there is little written evidence to support this. She apparently engaged in political discussions quite often and was in contact with a certain Otto Hübener, later murdered by the Gestapo for his activities in the Resistance. In *The Turning Point*, Klaus portrays how in Vienna, in 1932, Annemarie was enraged when the conductor Toscanini was slapped by the fascists:

> This fascist vermin! Just because he didn't want to play their idiotic national anthem! And no one protests against this outrage! Everything carries on in Venice, in Italy and in Europe as if nothing has happened! It's enough to drive you crazy!

Life also carried on in Berlin 'but its prevailing peace had something tragic about it' (Simone Weil).

Day and nightlife in Berlin

Schwarzenbach lived in the elegant Westend district of Berlin, at first with Maria Daelen, a friend and a doctor and later a delegate to the Council of Europe. Her first address was in Königin-Elisabeth Strasse; later, she took a flat of her own in the same area. At the very beginning of her stay, she lodged in Berlin Frohnau with her cousin Elisabeth

Albers-Schönberg, one of Chief Commander Ulrich Wille's daughters.

And what did she do? 'She lived dangerously. She drank too much. She never went to bed before sunrise' (Ruth Landshoff-Yorck). This is an exaggeration. Of course, nightlife in Berlin was different and more exciting than in Bocken; the ever-present riding whip of her mother was reduced perhaps to a harmless prop in a local bar act. As depicted in *Lyric Novella*, she went to clubs and the theatre and frequented gay and lesbian bars such as Mali und Igel and perhaps El Dorado. In those West Berlin bars, she came across her own reflection because 'there, the androgynous ideal was celebrated' (Wolfgang Theis, Andreas Sternweiler). Often, she went to the cinema and watched films like Cocteau's *The Blood of a Poet* or Eisenstein's *Battleship Potemkin*. She wrote about films; alongside reviews of Cocteau and *Blonde Venus* (she probably met Marlene Dietrich), she wrote an article about a visit to the UFA studios and on 'Film Direction and Filmscripts'. The premiere of *Girls in Uniform* at the Gloria Palast on 27 November 1931 must have been a highlight for her: it was based on a play by Christa Winsloe, a friend of Klaus, and Erika had a role. The story of an unhappy love affair between a pupil and a teacher in a home for girls would have reminded Annemarie of her own experiences at boarding school.

What else did she do? She was often out in her car or on horseback. Above all, however, she wrote, frequently 'inspired' by alcohol or gramophone music. In Berlin, she was 'completely possessed by a writing mania' (reflected in numerous pieces of writing, many of which are missing).

She also read the works of some of the most important writers both of the time, and of today, such as Proust, Kafka, Gide, Cocteau, Hemingway and Thomas Mann. Of her contemporaries, she seems to have been impressed by Irmgard Keun and chose to compare her talents with those of Gabriele Tergit and Katrin Holland. She was personally acquainted with authors such as Wilhelm Speyer, Karl Vollmoeller (who she had met in 1929), Annette Kolb, Bruno Frank, Thomas Mann and later Erich Maria Remarque. Like a mere handful of Swiss writers before the Second World War, she came into contact with modern literature and progressive forms of writing and was influenced by their respective social and cultural settings. That is why much of her writing is 'quite un-Swiss in its chic affectedness and cosmopolitan in its milieu' (Carl Seelig), having little to do with the Swiss literary tradition.

The power of friendship

Although Schwarzenbach had put a great geographical distance between herself and her family, nothing would allow her to entirely escape its 'spirit', ever-present in the form of her guilt as well as through the various 'emissaries' and 'branches' of the family in Berlin. To counter this, she tried to set up her own separate world with two circles of friends providing its pillars of support. One, the mainly homosexual circle around Erika and Klaus to which belonged the theatre set designer Mopsa Sternheim, daughter of the dramatist Carl Sternheim, and the journalist Doris von Schönthan, who was also friends with the authors Franz Hessel and Walter Benjamin. An entry in Mopsa Sternheim's diary talks about 'Annemarie's ethereal beauty and her dream'. Not least of all was Therese Giehse, the Munich-based actress who stayed in exile at the Schwarzenbachs' in Sils-Baselgia, Switzerland, and who was supposed to have looked after Annemarie like a mother.

The other circle of friends comprised mostly women, such as the doctor Maria Daehlen. There was also the journalist Ursula von Hohenlohe with whom Schwarzenbach was deeply in love; it was she who prompted Schwarzenbach to write *Lyric Novella* with her words: 'I make it too easy for myself and it's a pity' (1931). The writer Ruth Landshoff-Yorck was there too; she wrote a portrait of Schwarzenbach and published a poem that read like a homage to her friend in need of consolation: 'As you know that I can console you / You call trouble everywhere to your aid / And send it off to fetch you consolation' ('For You', 1935). Then there was the art historian Hanna Kiel, author of a volume on sculptor Renée Sintenis. (Schwarzenbach was perhaps on more intimate terms with the lesbian-leaning Sintenis, full of admiration for her Sappho illustrations or graceful horse sculptures). This clique also included Lisa von Cramm, who was married to the German tennis champion Gottfried von Cramm and who belonged to the circle around the Rot-Weiss tennis club in Berlin. The photographer Marianne Breslauer, former pupil of Man Ray, became a chronicler of this group, entering its bounds by shooting a series of its member's portraits. She intended to repeat the process every five or ten years to document the changes in their lives but she emigrated from Germany in 1936 and thus could not complete her project. Most of her portraits of those women look as if they were taken yesterday, and the 'modernity' of their appearance can be understood in the light of the following comment by Breslauer: 'We all dressed alike: masculine, short hair, styled to look like lesbians without actually being so.' The melancholic Schwarzenbach must have felt like a foreigner among these vivacious women but this circle of female friends formed a barrier that protected her from the dominant and sometimes threatening male world.

Although it did not prevent her from writing 'we are lost girls in the woods', a description most true for herself than perhaps the others at the time.

'Im Bann von See und Reich'
(*Under the spell of lakes and empires*)
(*Karl Haushofer*)

'At home, everybody rides horses. One brother takes part in horse-riding tournaments. The mother too. She certainly wants Annemarie to take more interest in horses, to ride in tournaments' (Landshoff-Yorck). So the obliging Annemarie kept up her riding, quite willingly, in Berlin. She was riding in 1933 when Hitler came to power, cantering circles in a riding arena in the company of 'Frederician soldiers, as colourful and upright as porcelain figurines' but who had no live ammunition. Inside, the eerie, fragile rococo world; outside, the Nazis made of Krupp steel. And Schwarzenbach trotting and galloping on her horse, wanting to leap over every obstacle that loomed in her path.

She would, every now and then, be visited by members of the family (they rode too). She occasionally went home to Switzerland, both to allay her homesickness and to research her contributions to two volumes on the country. She also stayed in touch with her cousin Elisabeth Albers-Schönberg in Berlin Frohnau. Sometimes she would meet, also in Berlin Frohnau, Albrecht Haushofer, whose father Karl was acquainted with the Schwarzenbach and Wille families. The talented writer Haushofer was a professor of geography and geopolitics in Berlin, and a collaborator, from 1934 to 1938, at the *Dienststelle Ribbentrop* (Ribbentrop Office), a National Socialist organization that dealt with foreign policy matters. Schwarzenbach must certainly have met him at the homes of her relatives. He greatly admired her and allegedly even proposed marriage in 1930. Haushofer, who swayed between resistance and conformity in his attitude to the Nazis, must have identified with Schwarzenbach, not least because she had a similarly ambivalent relationship to Germany. Connected by family and intellectual ties to politically conservative circles, as well as to Germany's cultural heritage, both Haushofer and Schwarzenbach were not able to abandon the country entirely, even during its most sinister era. At the end of the 1930s, Haushofer began to organize 'an antifascism, motivated mostly by conservatism and an intellectual aristocratism' (Eike Middell). Around 1942, he allegedly considered murdering Hitler. On 20 July of the same year, he was arrested on charges of fraternizing with insurgents and incarcerated in Moabit prison. Shortly before the end of the war, he was shot on a field of rubble in Berlin. His body was found with blood-spattered sheets of poems that were later dubbed 'The Moabit Sonnets'.

'Wie wurden Dir die jungen Jahren schwer' (How heavily your youth weighed on you) wrote Haushofer in

'Traumgesicht' (Heavenly Face), a sonnet dedicated to Schwarzenbach. The reason it weighed so heavily on her was partly because her notion of love had no ideological boundaries. She later expressed this in Africa when she said: 'Love begins when one can love one's enemy.'

As resolutely as she fought the Nazis as a political power, so too was she drawn to women connected through their husbands to conservative, even reactionary, circles. Sometimes, this proved to be a test of endurance in her relationship with the Mann siblings. A certain Frau von Schmidt-Pauli, for instance, was one of Schwarzenbach's 'great consolers' in Berlin, as well as Maria Daelen and Ruth Landshoff-Yorck, when she, as her fellow countryman Robert Walser twenty years earlier, was afflicted by 'loneliness of a terrible kind' (Walser). Schmidt-Pauli appears as 'Frau von Niehoff' in *Lyric Novella*; her husband, Edgar von Schmidt-Pauli does not make a favourable impression in the book. Schwarzenbach must have seen through him, for Schmidt-Pauli published a book in 1933 on Hitler. Klaus described him in the same year as a 'blackmailer': 'Nazi writers have him represent them at home and abroad' ('Drinnen und draussen').

In Berlin, Schwarzenbach was literally under the spell of 'lakes and empires', as Karl Haushofer summarized in 1925 in relation to the situation of the Swiss writer C. F. Meyer, who, like Schwarzenbach, had lived on Lake Zurich. How could she shake off this spell? 'Flucht nach oben' (Upward Flight) is the significant title of a lost novel from around that time but 'up there' awaited the long arm of her ancestors.

In *Lyric Novella,* the narrator reads the names and deeds of courageous Prussian officers inscribed on an obelisk near Rheinsberg Castle. General von Zieten's inscription would have impressed Schwarzenbach: 'He was victorious in every combat. [...] But what put him above all others was his loyalty, his selflessness and his contempt of all those who gained wealth at the costs of downtrodden nations' (From the French by Theodor Fontane). The discouraged narrator is dumbstruck by such heroism and wishes he had a sword with which to feel the strength and confidence of his ancestors and to protect himself from his own uncertainty. But there is no sword: Schwarzenbach can only 'draw' her pen as a battle weapon. The world of her ancestors, the validity of their order, has been cast in stone. What remains are their names, their language. Schwarzenbach remains alone, not at home by the lake, nor in the past, nor in the future 'empire': the Third Reich.

'Ich halt's nicht aus, ich halt's halt's, halt's nicht aus'
(I can't bear it, I can't, can't, can't bear it)
(Klaus Mann)

In January 1932, Annemarie wrote to Erika that 'One should leave Europe and the old ways for a while; too much courage and too much patience is required of us here.' In approximately the same month, she finished *Aufbruch im Herbst* (Departure in Autumn) and *Lyric Novella*. In both, much is questioned and lamented and, through the downward spirals of pessimism and desperation, love is sought and attempted. The writer's identity crisis was manifested in these endeavours, and intensified by the increasing radicalization of everyday politics which deeply shook both her faith in Europe's cultural uniqueness and her strength to survive. In a similar state of existential uncertainty, Klaus Mann published in spring 1932 his novel *Treffpunkt im Unendlichen* (Meeting Point at Infinity) about the 'loneliness and helplessness' (Frederic Kroll) of a group of young artists and intellectuals. Two protagonists attempt to flee but end up in a nightmarish, hashish-induced trip to North Africa (an incident based on the siblings' traumatic drug experience in Fez, 1930).

Despite the historical upheavals around them, both Klaus and his Swiss friend longed for new experiences in foreign cultures. No doubt they hoped a long expedition would also enable them to collect material for a book. The fact that he and his friends would write books that would 'often be set on journeys' or in foreign countries was clear to Klaus in as early as 1927. He put this aspiration into practice when in 1929 he published *Alexander*, a book about Alexander the Great. Perhaps this manuscript was the impetus for a road trip that the siblings planned to Persia in May 1932, along with Schwarzenbach and their friend Ricki Hallgarten. Or perhaps they were inspired by the sociologist and writer Leo Matthias, who met Schwarzenbach in the spring of that year in Berlin and who was the author of *Griff in den Orient. Eine Reise und etwas mehr* (Reaching into the Orient. A Journey and More) which recounted his travels in Persia. A sentence from his book anticipates the distressing experiences that Schwarzenbach was to have in that country: 'Persia has all the deserts in the world, and more.'

Persia was, at first, a nightmare for Schwarzenbach: the day before they were due to leave, Hallgarten committed suicide, a terrible shock for the three remaining members of the trip. Then, instead of travelling east they went south, to Venice. The 'Moorish magic of its architecture' (Klaus Mann) would have to provide a substitute for the desert but even a romantic gondola trip did not give Schwarzenbach peace of mind. For, as Klaus describes in *The Turning Point*, her mother, infuriated at the defeat of one of her show-jumping horses, accused her daughter on the telephone yet again of having 'no moral footing and [being] full of base instincts'.

Schwarzenbach lost her footing even further when, some months later, she grew addicted to narcotics. She was introduced to morphine in Berlin either by her friend Mopsa Sternheim or because of an illness or after a car accident. Just as she was addicted to Erika and her mother's love, just as the young man in *Lyric Novella* was to Sibylle, so too was she to the drug. Her tremulous faith in her own undeveloped potential was often intimidated by the personalities of Berlin's so-called intellectual giants. She would have agreed with the Swiss writer Friedrich Glauser, also a narcotic addict, when he wrote: 'Only those who suffer greatly from feelings of low self-esteem take morphine' (*Morphium*). Or did she grow curious while reading *Treffpunkt im Unendlichen*, in which morphine-addict Klaus refers to the drug as 'Urmutter Mo' (Mother Goddess Mo) and speaks of its 'great consolation, wonderful consolation' which, unfortunately, has the 'slight side effect' of 'destroying some within a year'. 'Shocking dejection' (*Freunde um Bernhard*), her hypersensitivity, her overwhelming feelings of responsibility which later took on a sociopolitical dimension: all these sometimes made life unbearable for Schwarzenbach. Why not seek relief through a short trip to another, simulated world? 'I don't enjoy thinking. Some day I will want to forget everything,' she noted as early as *Freunde um Bernhard.*

The extent to which the pressure of the political situation influenced her descent into a comatose state is evident in her behaviour when Hitler came to power at the end of January 1933. Shortly after this historic event, she wrote to Erika:

> I had such a high, persistent fever that even Hitler's torchlight procession seemed far away and I remained indifferent to it, and once more I thought that for this reason and others, the state of being ill is gentle and a relief, like all states where one is partly lost in one's own world and where there is no desire or reason to take action.

Only by desensitizing herself, by playing dead, could she endure the thought of the brown-shirted hordes marching past and her mother's approval of them. The upper classes lay prostrate at Hitler's feet during that period, although they liked to believe that they were above him.

The novella—writing along the fault lines of appearance and reality

Schwarzenbach had been in Berlin for just over a month when she integrated her experiences of the city into her literature and wrote *Lyric Novella*. She travelled to Rheinsberg, near Berlin, in November 1931, 'in darkness, completely against my will and flying in the face of my cowardice' after an unhappy love affair with a woman. Once there, she 'slept at once for fourteen hours, crying a few tears in-between out of loneliness'. In Rheinsberg or shortly after, she began writing the novella and finished it sometime around the end of 1931. The work was published by Rowohlt Verlag— presumably due to negotiations conducted by the Rowohlt writers Wilhelm Speyer and Ruth Landshoff-Yorck—a year a half later. This delay went on to have significant consequences for its reception. A non-political love story, it was interpreted as an escape from the events of 1932–33. When she gave a reading in St Gallen in January 1932, the audience could not have known that Schwarzenbach had almost completed her novel *Aufbruch im Herbst* (Departure in Autumn), which too she had begun in 1931. The review in *St Galler Tagblatt* is the only reference to the missing manuscript, and not only affirms the novel's spiritual affinity to the novella but also points to the latter's non-existent social aspect:

> The writer tackles problems courageously; she kicks against the inner turmoil that young people now suffer from. [. . .] She steps out of her social circle and into the world; she leaves the garden of the aristocracy behind and attempts to capture the spirit of the city's outer limits and the opposition.

Although Schwarzenbach describes her experiences in the novella as those of a young man, the autobiographical elements in her writing are unmistakable. Close friends and acquaintances are presented in a line-up of characters from the Mann siblings and Klaus' extremely young lover, Wilhelm Speyer to Elizabeth Albers-Schönberg to Schmidt-Pauli's wife. The setting is also identical: the narrator recalls, in rural Rheinsberg, his Berlin love affair with Sibylle, making notes and reflecting on his experiences just as Schwarzenbach did. Her interlacing and overlapping of real and fictional experiences, and her instant reaction to new experiences in writing, is a feature found in Klaus' work too. Even the process of writing had to be completed quickly: it was commonly known that Mann and Schwarzenbach wrote very fast.

Klaus had barely got to know Annemarie during that spring holiday in 1931 when he 'worked' the character of 'Annemarie' into his *Treffpunkt im Unendlichen*, which he finished in the summer of that year. Like the real Annemarie in Berlin, her fictional doppelgänger arrives in Paris wanting to learn and live a little. The naive girl sleeps with countless men and idolizes the thrillingly dynamic Greta, a former dancer. In Paris, sometime in 1928, Schwarzenbach had met the dancer Lena Amsel, inspiration for Greta's character, and dedicated a chapter in *Pariser Novelle II* to her.

It was only through the artifice of a literary character, through the medium of writing, in print, wherever possible, that Annemarie and Klaus seemed to become aware of their own reality and that of others. Their restless, fugitive lives, their almost transitional existence between sexes and generations could only be endured by their replication in writing. Bent over their sheets of paper, somewhat narcissistically, both writers shaped their reflections by joining words and sentences, desperately desiring to recognize themselves. The extent to which these 'methods' were influenced by appearance did not go unnoticed. Benjamin, for example, passed on a remark attributed to Speyer about the circle around the Manns: 'Their code of honour is to verbalize everything' and added, 'How deep their obligation towards appearance is.' This 'verbalization' was their only way of 'appearing to be assimilated'. Speyer worked through his interpretation of this feature in his *Sommer in Süden. Eine Liebesgeschichte* (Summer in the South. A Love Story, 1932) that reads like a counterpart to *Lyric Novella* and *Treffpunkt im Unendlichen*. Alongside the siblings, Schwarzenbach appears in it as a 'young writer of stunning beauty' and a 'lovely Sappho worshipper'. At the end of the book, the main character Aglai, based on the Manns' friend Eva Herrmann, says to her older admirer 'Wouldn't you rather [. . .] look at my picture [. . .] rather than me?'

Klaus and Annemarie, however, were equally fascinated by life and art, even if Siegfried Kracauer implies in his damning review of *Treffpunkt im Unendlichen* and *Kind dieser Zeit* (Child of the Times) that they and their friends were only interested in living for art: they 'plunder their experiences before they have taken hold of them; they amass experiences for the sole purpose of using them straight away and therefore gather nothing.' In Afghanistan in 1939, Schwarzenbach claimed that art was the only space where she could survive her greatest personal crisis: 'Truly, I only live when I write.'

Love as a meeting point at infinity? (*Klaus Mann*)

'I'm only alive when I'm hooked' could be the maxim of *Lyric Novella*: hooked on (family) tradition, hooked on love. Love as an attempt to kick the habit of tradition. But the title of her 1931 novel, *Aufbruch im Herbst*, signals

Schwarzenbach's will to change. In it, 'It is those who are lonely inside who want to kick the habit of whatever ties them down' (*St Galler Tageblatt*). They want to kick the habit but are afraid of the emptiness lurking in the unknown. If one were to kick the habit of the adored Sibylle, whom one can 'only die for in the end', one would no longer be able to see her. And as a writer, Schwarzenbach does not want to kick the habit: she would then no longer be able to describe the object of her desire. Her highly visual, non-reflexive style of writing requires the most painful self-reflection.

The puzzling figure of Sibylle, simultaneously intimate and distant, seems to be an incarnation of both Erika and Renée. She entices the young narrator and then retreats, thus becoming a figure of longed for but unattainable liberation. Is she not also a metaphor for the alluring world of Berlin to which Schwarzenbach succumbed? The inspiration for this character may perhaps have been a 'cool, cynical girl who served drinks in a bar, pouting but ruthless towards her fellow human beings. And towards Annemarie too' (Landshoff-Yorck).

The melancholic lover who wanders through the woods and the Rheinsberg palace gardens prefers to be the lonely hunter of his lover's heart. And on his hunt he is sometimes accompanied by a machine: his car. The car is the ultimate symbol of Schwarzenbach's restlessness as well as of her attempts to gain freedom. Her obsession with driving is displayed even in her writing technique: her often roughly sketched characters are observed as if from a passing car. The car is her *Wundertier* (fabulous animal) and she thinks of it with 'true tenderness'. It is her most loyal friend since it is always there, always waiting. In it, she can drive away from any and all decisions. A car as swanky and substantial as Schwarzenbach's Mercedes Mannheim was perhaps a protective shell for the upper classes as a protective shell to shield themselves from all kinds of change.

In *Lyric Novella* and in her other writing, love is yearned for more often than it is experienced. Intimacy between the protagonists is mostly short-lived, more a 'pressing' than a caress. There is always distance, or coolness. The partners rarely have equal rights; one is usually hopelessly dependent on the other. Such as, in *Lyric Novella*, the slavish devotion of the porter's son and Willy, of Magnus and even Sibylle. The officer's milieu of the Schwarzenbach family where one communicated with subordinates mostly through orders evidently played a significant role in the behaviour of her characters. Their actions are prescribed, and freedom in love is mostly out of the question.

Relationships between lovers scarcely develop, as if the writer were scared of the consequences. Love too, it seems, is an action in life like any other, having 'thousands of consequences', 'terrible responsibilities' and where 'no judgement is right or correct' (*Lyric Novella*). The moral and ethical scruples of the writer lie beneath the same sword of Damocles of the twice quoted, 'terribly simple, terribly true refrain' (Klaus Mann), 'Mankind is to be pitied,' from Strindberg's *Dream Play*. How to manage love when it's 'not easy' to be a 'human'? (Strindberg). Merz' words echo from the past, the 'most beautiful words' from her confirmation in 1925: 'And if I have prophetic powers, and understand all mysteries and all knowledge, and if I have all faith, so as to move mountains, but have not love, I am nothing' ('The Hymn to Love', 1 Corinthians 13:1–4). Schwarzenbach's hymn to love from 1935 went: 'Of course you know that no one, even for the shortest possible moment, can penetrate the heart of the other and unite with him.' Despite this, we 'have no other consolation other than to love and stand by each other' (*Death in Persia*). Like Klaus, she held on to the 'ethos of non-possession' in love (Kroll). Since 'I have never been more open, more ready than when I had to part from a beloved friend' (*Conversation*). Where does one meet them? At infinity?

'I only love the language of a book'

If something is truly modern in *Lyric Novella*, then it is its language. Clear, simple and very rhythmic, its dispassionate tone is set against the narrator's lyricism and thus creates a tension. A slightly ironic undertone can be detected at times, unusual for this author and not found in any of her other works. There is virtually no world present other than the peaks and troughs of the young man's feelings and their reflection in the landscape. Minimalist writing in the positive sense of the word, the writer describes only what she is experiencing at that moment. This was why Schwarzenbach was not able to a create a literary reality out of the social circumstances in which she found herself. It was only later in the stories from the Orient (1934–35) that she attempted to do so.

The degree to which the exceptional language of the writer was acknowledged is evident in the comments on the novella and the two missing novels. Klaus praised it thus in his review of the novella: 'The style has a lightness, an aroma and a rhythm' and is 'taught by the best Americans, for example Hemingway.' The *St Galler Tageblatt* mentions the 'exemplary use of language' in *Aufbruch in Herbst*. 'The style [. . .] reveals rigorous asceticism [. . .] No gimmickry is to be found anywhere, no concession to the currently established allures of fashion.' The *Neue Zürcher Zeitung*, after Schwarzenbach's reading in Zurich from *Flucht nach Oben* (July 1933), referred 'to the musical enchantment of sounds that sometimes touches one's innermost feelings.' For Schwarzenbach, therefore, the structure of a text was in the movement and nuance of its language. What she said about *Pariser Novelle II* was also true of *Lyric Novella*: 'I only love the language of a book. It can be about trivial things, or even better, about nothing. I don't want to write reports. Actions are not important: I want to actually experience them or do them myself.' This also reads like an anticipation of the criticism that was made of her works—that they were lacking in plot, that they were superficial. Had Schwarzenbach been self-critical, however, she would have admitted that, in some of her writing, her language lacked the right movement and structure.

'It is a paradox to write the tragedy of a young man'

Why did Schwarzenbach cloak her feelings towards a woman with a heterosexual love story? Did she want to distance it from herself? Or did she want to be supported by the strength and self-confidence of the traditional male narrator? The man in the novella, whose behaviour could be described as 'feminine', bears the characteristics of Schwarzenbach's androgyny. And the reader is left with a puzzle.

If we take the author literally, she is able to split her self into various personalities in a book. In *Pariser Novelle II*, she writes: 'If I wanted to write a book, I would cut the report of a murder out of the newspaper and read it ten times. And then I would begin to fall in love with the murderer [. . .] and then the woman he murdered, and the woman would have a little child who I'd also love, and then I could begin to write the book.' Thus Sibylle in *Lyric Novella* is part of Schwarzenbach's personality, and the exploits of the narrator cannot necessarily be traced back to the biography of the author alone: every experience is transformed by language into another, and real personalities are transformed into figures of speech.

Schwarzenbach's masking of her homosexuality in most of her writing had to do with the behaviour of her mother: if Renée was already 'offended' by the two entirely harmless books that Annemarie wrote about Switzerland, then her reaction to the almost morbid subjectivity of the novella was probably even more censorious. As if conforming to her mother's objections, Schwarzenbach's next book, *Winter in Vorderasien* (Winter in the Near East, 1934) was relatively impersonal. Perhaps it is no coincidence that her writing on unequivocally lesbian themes—*Pariser Novelle II* and *Death in Persia*—remained unpublished at the time. It is likewise no wonder that apart from one, all other poems from this period are missing. The one surviving poem, *Krankenhaus-Nacht* (Night at the Hospital, 1933) contains the following lines: 'Ich träume ich liege neben Dir— / Derselbe sanfte Rausch umgebe uns, / Dein Arm um meine Schulter, / Schwesterlich / Der gleiche Atem trage uns.' ('I dream I am lying next to you— / The same gentle tremors envelop us, / Your arm around my shoulder, / Sisterly / The same breath carries us.') As early as 1928, Schwarzenbach admitted in a letter to Merz that 'I have never felt a warm, powerful attraction, the searing sensation of friendship, all the young, glowing strength in me, for any other than a woman, I can only love women with true passion.' The theme of the military aspect of the Schwarzenbach clan was evidently taboo as well: the novel *Flucht nach Oben*, which was presumably destroyed by her mother, partially deals with the suicide of a young army officer whose brother recognizes 'ecstatically, in the fading expression of the suicide victim, his own face; but no sooner has he seen it than it is taken away again' (*Volksrecht*).

Physiognomy of a Hitler assassin?

Like love in Schwarzenbach's writing, her characters too rarely develop. Out of sheer consideration towards others, they do not manage to fulfil their own desires, much like the author, and are stricken by their lack of joy in life. At the same time, they desire this emptiness, this state of impotence, for they believe that they hear the voice of their lives more strongly in their lament. And so Schwarzenbach cultivated her 'pose of pain' (Klaus Mann) in which she could be in touch with herself. Her face often seems like an icon of grief and seems to be many miles away from her beating heart. It is perhaps for precisely this reason that she seemed to be a 'strange incarnation of far-reaching sorrow' (Hugo Mettler) for many young people in search of meaning at the time.

In his novel *Symphonie Pathétique* (1935), Klaus describes how, after Tchaikovsky's death, a grief-stricken youth, leaning against a wall, wishes he could petrify there as a 'Figure of a Lamenting Youth'. Unaware of this description, Breslauer, in 1938, photographed Schwarzenbach in a similar pose in front of a wall in Sils. The resulting two photographs echo the painfully tense faces of the girls and boys, frozen in eternal youth and appear in photographs that hang on the wall of the adult Gérald, a 'life guide' in *Freunde um Bernhard*. They are still-lifes. Like many characters in Schwarzenbach's writing, with their narrow shoulders and hips, they resemble statues, reminiscent of the infirmity in Giacometti's figures. With their 'youthful smoothness and slenderness', however, they are receptive, like antennae, to 'distant promises', and have something utopian about them. Some of these figures, with their serious expressions and sometimes 'courageous brows', convey a grim determination. The mixture of earnestness as an attitude to life and an aesthetic pose is typical of the young men who idolized Stefan George (Robert Boehringer's *Mein Bild von Stefan George*, My Image of Stefan George, illustrates this strikingly). One of the members of this circle around George was the young Claus von Stauffenberg, who later attempted to assassinate Hitler.

So goes one story. Once, Schwarzenbach stood in the foyer of a Berlin opera house, presumably before 1933. Suddenly, Hitler appeared and walked past, very close to her. If

Schwarzenbach had had a revolver, she would have been able to shoot him. She regretted not having one, because she would have most certainly shot him. It is therefore not surprising that, at the University of Zurich, her classmates were in the habit of calling her 'Judith, after she slayed Holophernes' (Hugo Mettler). Even in 1940, in a letter to Klaus, Annemarie asked herself whether 'every individual quite determined to "take action" should not attempt to murder Hitler?' If only 'every action were not a burden'.

'One cannot turn one's back on Germany'

A new chapter began in Schwarzenbach's life when she declared her allegiance to the opposition in a letter dated 8 April 1933 to Klaus, who had emigrated shortly before. Her definition of opposition was expressed not so much by a desire to enter combat as a concern about the preservation of German or Western cultural heritage, to which she felt a deep connection: 'One cannot turn one's back on Germany—that would mean overestimating the freedom of the individual. Opposition does not entail taking flight or turning away and certainly not Pharisaic contempt—but maintaining the intellectual values that one believes in until a better time arrives.' Shortly afterwards, she left Germany and only returned a few times. With Klaus Mann and René Crevel, she planned to publish a journal for emigrants in Zurich. Instead, she financially supported her friend's journal *Die Sammlung*, which was published in Amsterdam and on which she worked a few times. In May 1933, she travelled with Breslauer to Spain, representing the real start of her life as a journalist. And everywhere, whether in Berlin or elsewhere in the world, she went through the same experience: 'There is nothing left. A dark street, my car, me. The night is infinitely empty' (*Pariser Novelle II*).

Roger Perret
Zurich, June 1988

Note

1 The Wandervogel was the first youth movement in Germany. It began in 1896 as a group of pupils at the Steglitz Gymnasium, Berlin, who went on country hikes and soon caught on all over the German-speaking territories (including Austria and Switzerland) although there were regional differences. Girls were admitted from 1904. Its members were interested in developing their own lifestyle (including their special dress, folk dance and music, nature trails and camp life) and aimed at autodidactism and creativity (*Selbsterziehung* and *Selbstgestaltung*). It is sometimes regarded as a forerunner of progressive education (*Reformpädagogik*) and naturism (*Freikörperkultur*) and core elements formed the scout movement in 1926. It was banned in 1933 in the course of the *Gleichschaltung* (political conformity under National Socialism) but groups re-formed after 1945.